NEW RULES FOR INCOMPETENTS

NEW RULES FOR INCOMPETENTS

DEAD EVIL MERCENARY CORPS™ BOOK 5

MICHAEL ANDERLE

DISRUPTIVE IMAGINATION

LMBPN Publishing
PMB 196, 2540 South Maryland Pkwy
Las Vegas, NV 89109

Version 1.00, July 2022
ebook ISBN: 979-8-88541-726-6
Paperback ISBN: 979-8-88541-727-3

THE NEW RULES FOR INCOMPETENTS
TEAM

Thanks to our Beta Team:
John Ashmore, Rachel Beckford, Kelly O'Donnell, Malyssa
Brannon

JIT Readers

Zacc Pelter
Jeff Goode
Dave Hicks
Peter Manis
Diane L. Smith

Editor

SkyFyre Editing Team

DEDICATION

REMEMBERING JUDAH RAINE

Judah was a very strong advocate for the Zoo, a Sci Fi Universe created by Michael Anderle. (Why travel to a distant star system when you can visit an alien jungle here on Earth?). Judah took it upon herself to create an author's guide to help new authors to the Zoo get up-to-speed quickly. She enlisted several readers to help create the author guide, what she ultimately referred to as the "Zooclopedia tyrranica." It truly was a monster spread-sheet, which was appropriate for all of the alien mutant monsters that roamed the Zoo. We had a lot of fun creating mutant, hybrid monsters and coming up with crazy names for them.

Since the Zoo was surrounded by militaries from a number of different countries, we needed to research what military hardware and weapons each country would use to make the stories realistic. We're pretty sure that researching all the different weapons got us listed on a least one NSA watchlist - or three.

Besides being a reference for new Zoo authors, Judah

also played a key role in creating new stories for several, very popular Zoo series. She made the stories fast paced, entertaining and fun. Those books were always popular with our JIT proofreading group.

Hashing out Zoo storylines, mutant alien monsters and technology was a lively affair generating lengthy on-line discussions. Due to the time differences, those discussions usually didn't start until after 10:00PM Eastern time and could last until 1:00 or 2:00 AM. After a while, my wife made me mute the channel so she could sleep. (I guess that was better than her telling me to go to another room.)

Judah always showed her compassion, wit and sharp intellect during our discussions. She challenged us, grounded us and supported us so we could help the new authors and help make the Zoo stories the most entertaining and fun stories they could be.

I'll never forget our late night discussions, Judah's compassion, drive and wit and our Zoo family that grew out of our common interest in this Sci Fi Universe. She will be missed.

Written by John Ashmore, a valued member of the LMBPN Beta and JIT teams.

CHAPTER ONE

They were heading right into the thick of things—as usual.

Chill couldn't complain, though. The folks in Coil Cove were still looking to them to lead, so they would be the tip of the spear. Better them than those with lesser equipment.

"I never thought there would be a time when I wished we had bad equipment," she admitted, dropping down to one knee to give herself a breather and check on her equipment behind cover.

They had forced their way closer to one of the Scourge's Nests, clearing out the external defenses as they went. This was the first time they'd been able to get close. In the nests, as they discovered, the Scourge produced the creatures they were fighting, as well as sent most of the signals controlling those creatures. Nobody could tell if the signals originated in the nest, though.

Being on unexplored ground was thrilling in its own way, but it also meant they were discovering the secrets of the Scourge alongside the people who had been on the station for a lot longer than they had.

"What, would you prefer it if we had to wait for someone else to get a decent shot?" Kortez asked, falling behind cover next to her and checking his suit. His was covered in more shit from the creatures he'd been bowling over than hers was.

"Being the first ones into the fight is always going to be a high-risk, high-reward situation." She patted her rifle. "Sure, we decide how and where the fight will go down, but we'll have to see it through, good or bad."

Kortez tilted his head and looked for Ivan. The third member of their team was setting up on a higher point that overlooked their advance. He would deal out damage while they drew the Scourge's attention. It was odd that he wasn't adding anything to the discussion. Chill assumed it was because he was too focused on giving them cover to join in.

"We could probably let the rest of the locals push in," Kortez suggested, not for the first time. "There are a lot more of them, and they've been fighting the Scourge for longer than we have."

"Using them as cannon fodder isn't the best way to keep their confidence up." Chill shook her head as she peeked out from behind cover, watching for any sign of the Scourge pushing back. "Besides, this is the first time we've come upon an intact nest. I want to have a look at what they're doing in there."

The other nests they'd found—three of them—had been vacated and left empty of anything they could use against the Scourge. That was why they'd decided to rush this nest once they'd picked up on where the signals were coming from. The hope was if they pushed hard and fast enough, they would be able to reach the nest before it was taken apart and moved.

Chill doubted whether they would find a monster factory up and running when they rushed in. They wanted to learn everything they could about their enemies, but it had been a risky plan from the get-go.

They were committed now, though. They were on the doorstep of the nest and waiting for the Scourge to fight back. She wasn't sure why it hadn't already tried to push them back. There had been the usual amount of resistance they'd come to expect from their enemies, but nothing had surged up to stop them from reaching the nest.

That was either good news or *really* bad news.

"Are we set up, Ivan?" Chill called. She got back a green checkmark on her suit's HUD, which told her their backup was ready. That had been the secret of their initial success in pushing the monsters back: driving their point of the spear forward, drawing most of the Scourge's attention, and opening space for their allies to set up with over-whelming firepower.

Ivan was their connection with the rest of the crews. He let them know where to set up while Chill and Kortez pushed in. He'd helped them from a distance as well, between his knives and the coilrifles.

He was still the technical expert with the mech suits, but Chill and Kortez felt like they were getting better at handling the damn things with every day they spent inside.

Chill assumed Ivan hadn't shouted any orders at them all day because he didn't have anything to add. She was still a long way from feeling like the suit was a second skin, but she was getting there.

"Time to move." Kortez pushed up and peeked around the pillar they were hiding behind. He shot a couple of rounds.

When Chill came out, it was clear that if the Scourge was going to try to stop them, their defenses would be waiting inside the nest they were approaching.

The map told her she was approaching a Vert civilian housing section. But the schematics picked up from the Jindahin's servers were hundreds of years out of date. After all that time, the Scourge might have recalibrated the whole area. They were intelligent enough to set up proper defenses and funnel a large-scale attack into choke points by shutting off selected openings in the areas under their control.

But they had been fighting the local crews for so long that they weren't prepared for anything approaching them with the firepower Chill and Kortez were bringing into play.

A handful of the smaller creatures stepped out, rushed forward, and tried to slow them down, but Kortez was having none of it. He bellowed out a battle cry Chill had never heard before and poured out rounds to thin the front lines before he crashed into them, forcing the bots to choose between retreating or being crushed underfoot.

Most of them chose to be crushed. Chill was getting used to the Scourge's odd tactics. Calling them "tactics" was overblown since they largely involved swarming anything and anyone who got close.

Chill tossed a couple of grenades deep into the backline to lessen their numbers as she and Kortez approached the entry. It was being sealed up to stop their attack, but there was no sign of any heavies to fight back.

She hoped the plan was to slow the attackers enough to allow the workers to clear the nest out. Since there were protectors in place, they had to assume the nest was still intact.

More Scourge made themselves known, popping out of holes in the walls and the structure around them. They tried to flank the crew, but Ivan and the other combatants were waiting for just that kind of tactic. They opened fire on the bots as they approached, making sure they couldn't support the defenses.

So far, it was working because the Scourge hadn't adapted to having the Dead Evil crew push in with heavy mech suits. They were only equipped to handle lightly armed and armored enemies who were on the defensive.

They had to hope the Scourge wouldn't adapt to the new variable that had been added to the Suneater Station. It had been working under the same parameters for the past hundred years with only slight variations, and so when humans showed up with better armor and weapons, it couldn't hold them off.

Chill knew better. Although she wanted to believe they were dealing with a run-of-the-mill AI from a hundred years ago, it had shown itself to be more than that—greater, more dangerous, and beautiful. Well, *Chill* thought it was beautiful, based on what little code she'd managed to get her hands on.

"Got movement coming from the right," Ivan warned them as they pushed toward the door. "Focus fire on the right, all of you!"

A half-dozen highlights on her HUD poured in from the people running on the backline as they started to push forward, telling her that the comm had been directed to the people rushing in to take up the space she and Kortez were clearing for them. They were careful not to get anywhere close to shooting their own people in the back, which Chill appreciated. Yes, it meant they needed to clear their own way through, but it was a good tradeoff.

"Keep moving!" Chill called, stepping forward when she saw Kortez lagging in his advance. It was her job to keep Kortez's enemies in front of him as he all but battered his head forward to clear the android monsters.

There were occasions when she needed to step in, and Chill was more than happy to do so, drawing her blade from the sheath on her hip. It was a new addition to her armor, thanks to the pirate crews on the station. She kept the coilrifle in her left hand and drove the blade into gaps in the armor of one of the heavier insectoid creatures, splitting it in half as she opened fire on the rest of them.

Her left hand wasn't her dominant one, but she could not miss at this range. Tungsten rounds ripped into a solid line of Scourge bots and passed through to the ones behind them.

"All good?" Chill asked, not daring to turn away from the front line as she pushed ahead of Kortez.

"Got something stuck in my leg," he growled back.

She took a peek at his vitals on her HUD, and the reading told her there were a couple of breaches in his armor. They were already being sealed, and he had no injuries that merited being reported.

Chill couldn't drive forward the way he did. Well, she

could if she wanted to, but her lack of experience meant she would open herself up to damage Kortez knew how to avoid. Well, most of the time.

Chill ducked as a pair of smaller bots jumped at Kortez and were driven back. She slashed at anything she could reach and shot blindly since if the barrel was aimed forward, she was going to hit something.

That was guaranteed, given the density of Scourge in front of them.

Kortez's suit started cooperating again, and he joined her push. Between the two of them, reaching the door was inevitable. Chill reacted to attacks within a meter from the mech on instinct. Alarms told her the suit had taken several breaches, but nothing it couldn't keep up with.

The door was nothing special, just another of a million installed on the station. It operated with hydraulics and sealed magnetically when there was a pressurization issue.

It didn't look like the Scourge had activated the magnetic seals, though. Instead, they were piling up crates and chunks of the station to block the pirate brigade.

It was not the most efficient way to go about it, but she respected the effort even as she tossed a grenade into the gap between the door and the wall. She pressed against the door to get cover from the blast.

The panel she was leaning against vibrated from the explosion inside. There was enough room created for Kortez to step through the gap between the wall and the door and push it open farther. They entered the nest together instead of filtering through one at a time.

The crates and boxes that had been piled up to block the entrance didn't hinder them. The Scourge had been intending to weld them in place to keep the attackers from advancing into the residential area.

There were plenty of structures inside the chamber, which had apparently been set up to house a few thousand settlers a very long time ago. The area looked decrepit since the buildings had been taken apart to construct a tower at the center. It was taller than the rest of the buildings.

It was considerably less familiar in its design as well. It had clearly been built by the Scourge.

"I think we have a winner," Chill announced as Ivan guided the other crews through the door, taking potshots at the Scourge creatures as they retreated. "Lights are still on, so it looks like it's still powered up."

"What are you thinking?" Kortez asked, raising an eyebrow. "Climb up to the top and see where the signal is coming from?"

"That or just get a decent look at what's going on inside there." Chill brought her suit around, reminding herself for the fiftieth time since they'd started out that as good as she was getting with the mech, it would still be a long time before she would feel comfortable in it. She needed to focus, or she would end up tripping over her own feet. "Ivan, what kind of scouting report are we looking at?"

He stopped organizing the troops to call up the data. "Looks like the Scourge has mostly cleared out their troops from the area, leaving behind only those required to defend and remove the bits and pieces of the nest. I would say that meant they didn't think we were coming or under-estimated how quickly we could move on them. Either way, I'll take it as good news."

"Oh, yeah, all good news," Kortez muttered. "No thought the bastards were priming us for a counterattack, right?"

"That's what Ivan and the other crews are looking for." She was stating the obvious while making sure Ivan knew what his job was. "We need to focus on pushing forward. Nothing more, nothing less."

Ivan nodded, motioning for them to get moving as he turned his attention back to the crews. They were setting up in defensive positions. That was their job, after all. They would move in after the Dead Evil crew cleared the space out for them and maintain the position so the spearhead crew had a safe point to retreat to when shit went badly.

So far, nothing had gotten that bad. Chill's working theory was that their first fight with the Scourge had stomped on their ambitions as well as sapped the resources they needed to create their creatures. In space, and especially on a station that hadn't been replenished in over a hundred years, resources were at a premium. Whatever was controlling the Scourge seemed to understand that dumping its soldiers into fights it wasn't prepared for wasn't a good idea.

If it was the case, they were looking at a slow, restrained retreat as the Scourge studied them, taking note of where and how they liked to fight while ceding control of an area.

They hoped getting their hands on an active nest would help them understand the process. There was also the hope of finding something out that would allow them to keep the Scourge on the back foot.

No one wanted to breach the tower they were

approaching. There was no telling what was waiting for them in there, and Chill had no intention of finding out until they had a better idea of what the antenna was doing at the top.

"Watch my back," Kortez muttered while firing at creatures who were trying to stop them.

Most of the Scourge had been thinned out. If the nest was going to launch any more for them to deal with, she wanted to have her feet firmly on the ground to blow them off Kortez as he made the plodding climb up the top of the tower. His mag boots would do most of the work, but it was still a slow and steady walk, with plenty of attack points for the Scourge to pour out of.

And they did.

"You've got movement coming your way," Chill called, highlighting the point they were coming from while trying to place her shots effectively.

More came from the left side, too. She drew her second rifle and shot at them. She didn't even need to land a kill shot. They were scrambling across the wall of the tower, meaning that a clip would be enough to knock them off and send them plummeting to the ground, letting the station's gravity do most of the work.

More came, drawn by sensors that detected Kortez climbing their building. The small swarm wouldn't have posed a risk had she and Kortez been together and on the ground. However, hanging off a tower and on his own, she understood why his body language told her he was panicking.

Worse, the bots she'd knocked to the ground weren't

out of the fight yet. Several, damaged from the fall but still functional, were dragging themselves over to her.

"Ivan, I could use a little help," she growled, her focus on what was happening above. The gamble was that even if Ivan couldn't help quickly enough, she wouldn't be able to hold off the attack on the climber.

If they attacked her too, she would have to defend herself rather than Kortez.

Kortez was three-fourths of the way to the top when something started gnawing on her thigh armor, trying to dig in. She dropped her rifle, yanked the creature clear, and stomped on its body while keeping her attention on what was happening on the tower.

"Almost there," she whispered, mostly to herself, although Kortez could probably hear her over the open comm. More creatures attacked, but before she could react, they stopped, and her rifle was pressed back into her hand.

"Keep going!" Ivan shouted, patting her shoulder. He sent more knives flying at creatures that had either survived their fall or were coming out of the bottom of the tower to attack her.

She kept her eyes on Kortez since he was still climbing. Chill continued to attack as he scrambled over the edge since she assumed there would be defenses waiting for him. He could probably do without more creatures coming at him from behind.

Ivan and the decky crews had her back, and the farther up the tower he was, the tougher it was to make her shots. Still, she'd found that the less she thought about shooting, the more hits she landed.

It wasn't until the rope zipped down to where she was

waiting for it that Chill stopped firing. She slotted the rope into the mechanism on her suit and it started climbing, picking up the pace to ensure she wouldn't be a sitting duck. The last time they'd scaled buildings, they'd learned to make sure they had a member of their crew covering their backs during the climb.

The first climb was always the most difficult. The second climber had help from the crewmate above to get to the top, making the ascent much faster.

She was halfway up when creatures poured out from inside the building. They had an odd sheen to their armor that told her they were freshly made, which she took as a great sign. Not fantastic since it meant they were attacking a building that was still producing defenses, but since it was still active, they would be able to get a peek at the systems the Scourge used.

Ivan covered her climb before joining them at the top of the building. Kortez reached over the edge to yank her up and attached a mine to the wall beneath her as creatures came up behind her.

"Nice work." Kortez paused when the mine went off, interrupting their attempt at conversation. "You getting the feeling this was a little too easy?"

Chill tilted her head as she approached the antenna. "You're the one who marched up a building with no help beyond what your suit provided with a bunch of mechanized horrors hot on your tail."

"They never got close," he admitted. "Have you and Ivan to thank for that. But yeah. Always nice to have your efforts be appreciated."

She smirked but switched her comm to the private

channel with Dorian. "Hey, kid, we're at an active antenna. You ready to put your skills to work?"

"I... Hey." Dorian cleared his throat, chewed, swallowed, and turned his mic on again. "Hey, boss. Sending the mechs in after wiping up the last of the stragglers left behind after your blitz. Putting them in sentry mode. It's ready on my end. You just need to connect the fob we worked up."

It had taken a lot of help from the decky crews to figure out a fob that would allow them to connect to any hardware the Scourge was using. Since they had been fighting them for a lot longer, Dorian surmised that over the years, they had figured out how to connect to what was attacking them. The kid had been right.

In theory, anyway. Chill doubted it would work, but there was only one way to find out.

"All right," she whispered and pulled the fob out of her pack. Its design was alien, although it did match the designs she'd seen on the building as she was climbing it and everything else they'd run into that was related to the Scourge. The group either had a central consciousness driving it, or it was the most efficient design the AI could come up with. They had many questions and only one way to get the answers.

"Don't worry," Dorian assured her. "I've isolated the device so that even if the Scourge attacks, they can't turn your mech or anything else on you. I'm keeping track of everything on this end. I've got the systems connected to the fob isolated, and I'm ready with a kill switch if those don't work."

"Sure," Chill muttered. "We're going to go ahead and underestimate the mechanical intelligence that has slowly been taking this station over for hundreds of years, shutting down any and all sentient attempts to slow it down or so much as settle on the station. That's not going to backfire on us in a massive way. Probably."

"Hey, I know what I'm doing. For the most part."

"Way to fill me with confidence."

Dorian spluttered, then cleared his throat loudly in her ear. "I got this. Just make sure nothing interferes with the fob while it's doing its thing."

She nodded. Kortez was fixing the damage his suit had taken. "All right. We'll keep the Scourge from interfering with the damn thing. Ivan, what's the situation look like down there?"

"No changes," Ivan told her. "Nothing to be worried about. Scourge critters moving around on the sides of the building, but it doesn't look like they're sure of what they're doing."

Chill glanced at the fob, then shrugged and plugged it into the slot that had been highlighted for her. Dorian might not have been following their movements through the area closely since his job was to have the empty mechs add to their firepower in the field. However, now that he'd focused on where they were, he kept pinging their systems and telling them the directions the Scourge was approaching from and in what numbers, as well as marking the sections of the antenna would work for their needs.

"Nope, that's just a power socket," Dorian muttered under his breath. "Try the one just above it. See if it works."

She did as instructed and the fob lit up blue, which told her they had hit the jackpot.

They weren't sure they wanted to win it, but they had to get more information.

"Oh, it knows." The kid sounded a little worried. "Not sure what it knows or what it is, really, but it's reacting to my intrusion. Not fighting back yet but putting up barriers. Wow, that's impressive."

"What is?" Chill snapped a shot at one of the creatures that was climbing up to deal with them. "Are we going to have incoming?"

"I'm not sure what I'm looking at, but I do know it's what we're looking for."

"You'll be uploading the virus?" Ivan asked.

"Calling it a virus is inaccurate," Dorian whispered, tapping on his tablet. "If anything, it's a countervirus. Whatever's been infecting the Scourge is a remnant from the viral attack we dealt with before. That's what the Over-Keeper said, anyway, and he spent lots of money acquiring the code for us, so I thought we might give it a try. See if he's onto something."

Ivan and Kortez were both looking at her like she was calling the shots. She appreciated that they put up a united front when they were in front of the deckies, but it wasn't going to fly when they were on their own.

"I'd appreciate some input from the two of you," Chill stated, trying not to sound like she was snapping at them.

"Seems like a good starter plan." Ivan shrugged, somehow keeping his suit from reacting like the person inside was having a seizure. "At this juncture, we might as well try the Over-Keeper's suggestions."

Kortez finished fixing his armor and straightened, then tried out the joints. "I agree."

It was as close to a consensus as they would get.

"Do it," Chill told Dorian. The fob's indicator light turned from blue to red. "I...what is this thing supposed to do, anyway?"

"It... Well, I hope it's going to neutralize enough of the nest's systems to allow me to run a hard reboot and purge everything." Dorian had a bad habit of sapping her confidence in their plans. "It might result in the whole of the Scourge going down for a while. More likely, it will keep doing whatever it was doing but attack only one node. This one. Whatever way it goes, you will want to make a quick exit. There is a lot of power going into the nest, so a big boom could be on the way."

"Shit." Ivan rolled his eyes. "You couldn't have told me that before I climbed the fucking tower?"

"I mean, sure." Dorian wasn't paying much attention to them now. "Should be pretty quick for you to go back down, right?"

"Something is wrong." Chill recognized the voice of one of the Over-Keeper's Janissaries. They had offered to assist with the attack, but the idea was still to keep the Jindahin from being tagged on the station, so she'd advised that it was best for them to hold off and be ready to support them if the proverbial fecal matter hit the ventilator.

"What's up?" Chill asked, moving to the edge of the building.

"Are you seeing this?"

It took her a moment, but then she did. The Scourge was still in the area, and they had the numbers to be a problem if they bunched up and attacked as one, but that was not what they were doing. A few were still crawling on the sides of the tower, while others were attacking the deckies and mechs. Most, however, were attacking each other and anything that stepped in front of them. Some were biting and tearing chunks off any buildings they ran into.

"That looks like the Madsong's effect on the Bugz, doesn't it?" Chill whispered. She zoomed in on a group of the larger creatures that were ripping into each other while the smaller ones joined in.

"It's uncanny," Ivan answered. "We need to get the fuck out of here."

"Not if they attack the Vert structures." Chill hefted her weapon. "We need to clear this area before they cause damage that'll wreck the station or make a hole that sucks us all out into open space."

"Fuck," Kortez hissed. "All right, let's get to work."

"Just another day in the office, eh?" Chill grinned as they started back down.

"Shut up."

CHAPTER TWO

The fight was different than they'd thought it was going to be. It *was* like the Bugz they'd fought that were affected by the Madsong devices. She couldn't help making the association. It was hard not to when the Scourge they ran into were fighting each other with as much ferocity as they fought the deckies and the Dead Evil crew.

The Janissaries had been forced to join the fighting. She wasn't pleased about it, but the Over-Keeper would have to understand that they were acting on a threat that would kill just about everyone in the Vert and could end up destroying the station.

Considering the core of his plan involved keeping the station intact, the Over-Keeper would have to understand that his people occasionally had to join the fighting. The Janissaries didn't need a justification for it, though. They were simple-minded—not because they were stupid, but because they were trained to view the galaxy in a rigid way. Enemies had to be killed. Allies had to be protected.

Missions had to be completed successfully. Their comrades had to get out of those missions alive.

Their training honed them into the weapons they needed to be, but what put them above and beyond all the other Jindahin soldiers, aside from the genetic manipulation that turned them into the finest fighters of their race, was that they *acted*. No morals, no deep thoughts. They were the first to pick up their weapons in any situation.

In this instance, they needed that level of enthusiasm.

"Got three more pockets!" Kortez called, highlighting the points. "Not big ones, but these are attacking the structure pretty fucking exclusively."

It was their kind of fight. Chill was pushing forward, rifle in her left hand and knife in her right. They would keep the station from falling to pieces around their heads. She was in her element. Years battling the Bugz, and here were more creatures that struggled and fought in the same way.

The galaxy was funny like that.

"Keep moving!" Chill shouted as she carved through the first of the pockets. Kortez and Ivan cleared the other two out just as quickly and efficiently.

And a little faster, if she was honest. Chill shook one of the Scourge corpses off her knife and ran over to a larger pocket of resistance. She had no idea how long it would take to clear them all out, but what they were doing was having an effect on the rest of the station.

The area's gravity suddenly went out. It usually did when there were power fluctuations, but she couldn't tell if those were caused by the damage the monsters were inflicting or the fob interrupting the programming. In either case, they had to sort it out and fast.

Stepping forward proved to be more complicated than it had been a second prior. The lack of gravity meant that where she had previously run forward, she now leaped forward with very little control over where she was going or how she got there.

It took a lot more effort to steady herself and lock her boots to the deck with the magnetic clasps. Kortez and Ivan needed to do the same. There was still gravity in the chamber, but it had dropped from one gee to a quarter-gee in seconds.

"Nope, did not need this today," she muttered under her breath. Her stomach rebelled at the idea of weightlessness. There had to be an implant or a medical procedure to deal with space sickness. She had to keep her mind focused on something other than her urgent need to hack her last meal up. There were plenty of distractions to help her with that.

"What the hell is going on?" Chill called over the comm while picking off a handful of the Scourge that hadn't secured themselves and were jumping up a little too high. "Dorian, I'm talking to you."

"I don't know." The kid's voice was annoyingly calm, which told her he was working the problem. "The readings I'm picking up make no sense. It looks like since the Serpent orbits and is orbited by a trio of dwarf stars, loss in gravity in just about any area of the station means you're being acted on by *that* gravity as well. The whole station needs to pump a lot more power into the grav systems than you would need anywhere else in space to keep people from being ripped apart by the triple grav pulls."

"So, what you're telling me is the grav systems on the Serpent are compromised?" Chill steadied herself and opened fire on another group of creatures.

"That is an understatement. I'm filtering through the readings now, and if I had to guess, this is a failsafe the Scourge set up in case we tried hacking into its servers. All the creatures have been programmed to detach from and jettison the compromised nest. I assume it's a defense to keep us from digging shit up, and it doesn't look like there's any priority to defend the structural integrity of the Vert area you're in."

It didn't tell them any more than what they already suspected, but it was good to have confirmation of those suspicions.

"We're going to cut the signal off, though, right?" Ivan shouted. He was doing better at managing the low gee than Chill was, nimbly alternating between using his mag clasps and moving freely. He used his mobility to wreck any Scourge creatures he encountered. "The antenna should be a pretty easy target at this point, and if we just cut off whatever signal is telling the bastards to keep ruining the Vert, they'll revert to factory settings, right?"

"It'll be a little more complicated than that," the kid assured him.

Kortez settled back down on the deck after an impressive leap. "Of course it'll be more complicated, but the principle is sound, right?"

"Not...not really?" Dorian was probably shaking his head. "The bots the Scourge creates are self-reliant, so when they get a signal, they continue acting on those orders until they get new ones. Interrupting the signal would leave them doing the same thing they already are."

"Could you send out a signal to stop them?" Chill suggested.

"I've been trying to replicate their signals' coding, but, well, that might take a little too long. Let's just leave it at that. With the deteriorating state of the area, it looks like the best option for getting everyone out alive and not losing the whole of the Vert is to shut the nest down. It'll send out one last blast that tells the bots to deactivate the way they did in the other nests."

"What about trying to mine the fucking nest for all the data we can get?"

"I'm working on it," he assured her. "But we have to consider the cost-benefit ratio of losing an entire fucking Vert. It's your call. There should be a power node at the base of the tower, so if you're going to blow shit up, I'd recommend Ivan apply his skills to that point."

"My skills?" Ivan raised an eyebrow.

"Your skills of destroying shit with a big bang, lots of smoke, and maybe a little fire?" Kortez offered helpfully.

"Ah. Yes, those skills."

Chill didn't like being forced into making the decision. This was their first chance to dig deeper into what the Scourge was doing on the station. Maybe find out what its plans were and discover how to stop it in one fell swoop. However, they had to make the play that would save the station, even if it stalled their efforts.

"We're blowing the node," she announced. She motioned for Kortez and Ivan to join her, and they kept shooting at the creatures that crossed their line of sight. "Dorian, could you—"

"Already sent you the node's location inside the tower and the easiest point of access. You might run into some trouble on the way in, though. There aren't any sensors, so I can't tell for sure, but it's right smack where the nests produce their bots."

"Thanks, Dorian. You're a doll."

"I'm a what?"

"I... Nothing. Never mind." It was an old saying, so old that she wasn't sure where she'd gotten it. It had just come out.

Better for them to just find a way out of the situation and move on.

"Cover me!" Ivan called as a small group of creatures converged on their position. There weren't many, but they came from enough points of attack to make it worrisome.

Chill claimed the points of attack she would defend, and Kortez took the other half. She made sure she hadn't accidentally picked the points fewer bots were attacking from. She would never hear the end of it.

Ivan donned his emergency atmo protection and climbed halfway out of his suit. As deft as he was with the fine motor controls of the mech, he needed to be hands-on with explosives. Since they were one wire cut away from losing the rest of the grav and the atmo in the chamber, he had to be prepared for anything.

He was vulnerable, so Chill and Kortez had to ensure that none of the creatures got into sniffing distance. Kortez could hold his ground, but Chill's most effective defense was to attack.

Her rifle heated up as she opened fire on the larger pockets approaching them. She cleared those out and turned her attention to one of the nimbler monsters. It was smaller than the common Scourge bots but lithe and agile. It jumped onto one of the buildings and jinked from side to side to keep her from getting a shot on it.

That one made her think a higher power was directing the bots to stop them or at least slow them down. When it came off the building a moment later, she dropped her rifle, drew her knife, and thrust it into the creature's chest as it tried to run around her.

After she pinned it to the nearest wall, Chill sent a tungsten round into the creature's head, smashing it. Having the vital wirework in one location was a design flaw, but she believed that was the point. The Scourge had a unique evolutionary design they reinvented as they met new enemies. It didn't have to make sense.

Fuck, humans and most sentient beings had the same design flaw, which arose from not *being* designed or exclusively evolving to survive combat. That was something they had to figure out as they went along.

"Get clear!"

Chill blinked. She'd slipped into a trance state where her body kept fighting while she thought. She was shooting better than usual, too.

She had come to believe her poor shooting skills were connected to her penchant for overthinking. After she worked through that problem, she would be able to contribute more to their long-range engagements. She might never be as good as Ivan or even Kortez, but better was still better.

What had Ivan said?

A shockwave hit her back. The suit took most of the damage, but she stumbled through the wall of a building that had partially collapsed over the years.

"Fuck!" She stepped out and shot the one Scourge that was still in the area.

"I told you—"

"You said to get clear," Chill interrupted Ivan. "Sorry. I was distracted and didn't react fast enough."

"All right, let's get inside." Ivan nodded for them to move through the hole he'd created. It was as close to a door as they would get. There were openings in the tower, but they were twenty meters up at the least. Some light made its way through them, and the creatures could slip out, but they were just elongated scribbles on the sides of the building.

There were no other windows or doors. Those openings were large enough for her to slip through with the mech suit, but what would be waiting for her on the other side? Best to make their own entrance.

Chill was the first one through. She stepped into a deep darkness her eyes could not penetrate. The sensors immediately painted her surroundings in infrared, showing a wide room whose ceiling was supported by a handful of pillars. Twenty meters up, the pillars branched out to the walls of the building—for support, she assumed. An explosion in the right place would bring the whole delicate construction down.

She knew where the right place was.

"Ivan, got the explosives ready?" she asked, highlighting the spot Dorian had indicated.

"Ready to go." He patted his pack.

"Can you put them on a timer?" Chill studied the building they were in, trying to ignore its raw beauty. "The blast will bring the whole damn thing down, and I don't want us to be inside when that happens."

Ivan nodded and got to work.

"Boss!" Kortez wanted her attention.

She turned around. Telling him to stop calling her boss would have to wait since there was something moving across from them. It was bigger than anything else they'd seen on the station.

"Open fire!" Chill shouted. She took her own advice and shot at the creature that was pushing up from below the deck. After more of its body emerged, she knew they didn't have the firepower to bring it down.

Dropping a building on its head would have to do the trick. They didn't have a lot of options.

"Ivan!"

"Yes, yes. Putting a fuse on the explosives." Ivan looked up from his work and corrected himself. "Putting it on a *short* fuse."

"That would be best. Run!"

Neither of the men had an objection to that. After Ivan set the timer, they made a beeline for the hole they had blown in the wall.

"Thirty seconds?" Kortez roared when the timer came up on their HUDs. "You only gave us thirty fucking seconds?"

"Less talk, more running!" Ivan advised.

Chill would have preferred to have more time to get out, but she understood his reasoning. They were more likely to survive a building dropping on their heads than a battle with the massive creature inside the tower, whatever it was.

The explosives went off, and the shockwave hit their backs just as they cleared the improvised door.

"Looks like all the feeds from the bots are down. Well done," Dorian announced. "Why...why did you cut the time to escape the building so short, though?"

"There was something big in there," Chill advised, then looked back. The building was not, as she'd hoped, coming down. "It's still in there. Still moving. Might be coming to attack us!"

"Oh. I didn't see any readings of it moving when you were in there."

"Well, it fucking was," Kortez growled. "And if the building doesn't come down...oh, there we go."

It was a slow process, but finally, cracks appeared on the walls as the structural supports failed, then the building came down.

Chill tilted her head. "We should—"

"Keep running, yes," Ivan advised. He grabbed the collar of her suit to get her moving again. The floor shook as the building collapsed behind them, sending pieces of steel and chunks of prefab in all directions. They were engulfed in a cloud of smoke and dust.

"Is it still there?" Kortez asked, slowing down and turning around.

"How the fuck should I know?" Ivan growled, although he too looked into the cloud of dust that engulfed them.

"We need to keep moving," Chill ordered, motioning for

them to go in front of her. "If that creature got out, we don't want to give it an easy target."

The station's air scrubbers had kicked in by the time they reached the deckies and the Janissaries.

"Notice anything?" Kortez commented, looking around.

"Grav systems are back online." Chill nodded. "The self-repair functions of the station must have fixed it first. Are any of you picking up movement from inside the dust cloud?"

No one indicated there was. After most of the dust was out of the air, it became apparent that whatever was inside had been disabled or switched off by the building falling on it.

"Shit." Kortez shook his head. "Just when you think you've seen everything this station has to throw at you, something else is waiting to ruin your day. I get the feeling we're going to have to deal with that bullshit every day we're here."

"Just another day in the life." She patted his shoulder and turned to the other crews. "All right, everyone. Salvage what you can, but we don't want to stick around long enough for the Scourge to think it's a good idea to launch a counterattack."

That was what they had been waiting for. The deckies had been scavenging and salvaging for decades, so they knew how to do it fast. They took off, leaving Chill and Ivan and Kortez with the Janissaries.

"What do you think it was?" Kortez finally asked. "If it wasn't connected to the nest network, it had to be something else, right? Maybe it wasn't part of the Scourge and they just built the building over it."

Chill shook her head. "My guess is it was a defensive measure they set up to fight anyone who tried to take the nest down. It wasn't on the network. Otherwise, it would defeat the purpose."

Ivan nodded. "That was my thought as well. We'll have to keep an eye out for them when we go after more nests."

He had a solid point.

Chill took a deep breath. They'd won this battle, and there was every chance they'd picked up data that would help them win in the long run. However, they had wanted to capture an intact nest to do research on. That was why they had pushed so hard and fast this time.

"We need to get back to Coil Cove," the Janissary captain muttered, nodding at his men. Fighting with the crews didn't mean they would stick around for the clean-up. He barked orders, and the Janissaries followed him back the way they'd come.

"Chin up." Kortez nudged her shoulder. "We pushed the Scourge back again. I'm calling this one a win." He and Ivan headed off to gather the deckies so they could return to their base.

"Yeah," Chill muttered.

"We won."

CHAPTER THREE

Coil Cove was a tremendous testament to how humans and other sentient species could settle in just about anywhere if they put their mind to it. That wasn't to say it wouldn't be difficult, but if they were persistent, they would get there...eventually.

There had been a lot of changes to the docking station since they'd made port there. Plenty of the decky crews were still active in and around the station, taking advantage of the vacuum left behind by the Scourge to start reclaiming the Verts. It was dangerous, especially considering that even with the Scourge being pushed back, they had left bits and pieces behind.

Still, they were reclaiming a substantial amount of salvage from the areas the Scourge was driven out of and using it to rebuild other things. With the rebalancing of power, Chill made sure the resources were distributed equally among the crews, and those working to turn the salvage into usable material would earn as much reward for their efforts as those picking up the salvage in the field.

It hadn't been her most popular idea, but she had been adamant that moving forward, they were all going to work together. There had been grumbling, mostly from the groups which brought the salvage back. They said they were the ones putting their lives on the line, but they were following the plan.

So far, it had worked out for them. Their defenses were better organized than they had been in the past, and the living spaces were split evenly between the crews.

If more crews arrived, they would have to expand out of Coil Cove into the areas formerly occupied by the Scourge. She assumed it would be a few months before interested parties gathered the resources, people, and ships required to journey to the Serpent. All they could do was keep advertising their work to get those who followed their adventures interested in joining them.

Kortez stated his worry that they might take advantage of people who were looking to them for work with the situation on Mugh-9 winding down. It was a fair point, but she reminded him that those same people had tuned in to watch the DEMC crew kill Bugz and thought it was entertaining. Fighting the Scourge wasn't as dangerous as killing Bugz, which meant that if they came here from Mugh-9, it wouldn't be difficult for them to adapt.

Chill *did* feel guilty. She had been dealing with it since they'd started working on the station. Their employer had his own agenda for the station once it was cleared and set up as the transport base for the nebula it bordered. His agenda had very little to do with the people already on the Serpent or those who would be joining them on it.

She would be in a better position to ensure the people

on the station would have a future on the Serpent after the Jindahin decided the place was usable. Since the current residents had experience working on the station, they would be the best people to keep it running.

The Over-Keeper would see that she was right, and if he didn't, she would make him see it, even if the Janissaries proved to be a problem. Maybe the time to talk to the Over-Keeper about the future of the people on the station was now. If so, she would get what he said in writing and display the agreement to the rest of the galaxy if he went back on his word.

It wouldn't slow him down if he planned to turn on them, but it would show him the consequences of fucking over the DEMC.

"Chill, you still with us?"

She'd have to control her habit of letting her mind wander. She shook her head and looked at Kortez and Ivan. Shoviil had joined them.

"I am now," she answered, pulling her helmet off. "How is life treating you, Shovie?"

"I asked you not to call me that," Shoviil muttered. "And all in all, not too bad. Alive and working, which is more than can be said about the rest of my crew. I was just asking Kortez and Ivan about the salvage from your latest venture."

Chill nodded. "There were...complications. Ran into trouble, so most of it is not in the best state. Up to you and the rest of the experts to determine if it was a good haul or not."

"We panicked when we ran into a creature we'd never seen in the station before," Kortez admitted. "Pushed the button and blew just about everything up to make sure we got *it* too."

"What kind of creature?" Shoviil smirked. He was watching the three of them carefully. "Can't say I'd believe three of you ran scared of anything the Scourge could throw at you. Many things, maybe, but not just one creature, even if it was new."

"You would understand if you saw it," Ivan grumbled.

"How would that change my perspective?"

"Because it was thirty meters tall at the very least," Chill commented.

"At the very least," Kortez agreed. "And so heavy, we could feel the vibrations from it moving. That said, we never got to see the whole creature."

"Seeing it wasn't the idea," Ivan cut in, shaking his head. "We could have gotten footage. Most of what we picked up was signature readings, although those readings alone were disturbing."

Chill nodded her agreement. "We were only looking at one creature, although it's possible there were more of them. Not sure if that would have been better or worse. It also wasn't connected to the network the rest of the Scourge was on, or it would have been acting the same way. Our tech support would have been able to spot it before we saw it in that case, too. It was big, and it was moving toward us in the dark. Not a lot of light in those nests. We blew it the fuck up before the rest of the monsters tore the whole place apart."

Shoviil narrowed his eyes. "I think I understand what you're saying. You ran into a new, terrifying side of the

Scourge and decided to blow everything up and ask questions later."

"Sounds about right." Ivan grinned. "I *am* proud of bringing that entire building down with one perfectly placed charge. It says a lot about the functionality of the buildings the Scourge is putting up. I bet I could write code for my HUD that would identify the weak points in a structure. Could *always* bring down a whole fucking building with one bomb if it's put in the right place if I had that information."

"I don't know. I've heard you can just use rocket fuel," Kortez muttered.

"What?" Ivan scowled at him. "No, you can't. That's a myth."

"We've had this conversation before. Remember when we called that expert?"

"Oh, yeah…your so-called expert."

"Not important." Chill rolled her eyes. "The point is the salvage coming might be iffy, but hopefully, the teams will come up with something. The people with us pulled out some stuff already, but the Vert is precarious. Grav and atmo systems have patches the station's auto-repair systems haven't addressed yet."

The Xo-Trang chuckled softly. "Well, I'll see what I can do to get the Vert repaired so we can do salvage ops in the area. Might be a while before anyone's interested, but if that makes the area safe, it's a good thing. It would require a fair amount of up-front investment to get the decky crews interested, though."

"You might want to wait on that, then." Chill sighed as he stepped out of his mech. As effective as they were in the field, it was tiresome to be in the suits. "We're going to have to secure financing from the Over-Keeper for that. I'll be damned if we'll put up money for his project."

"I see. Well, I'll wait for word before I ask for interest, then."

"Probably best, yeah."

Getting back to the ship meant working their way through the crews and groups watching them. Some waved and shouted Kortez's various battle cries. She'd tried to stop him, but he just couldn't help himself. He said he didn't like it when people copied him, but he couldn't help but break out in a giant grin when they did it.

That meant he was lying, but that was on him. Chill shook her head when they reached the ship. Dorian was waiting for them. Zichix was, too; the not-so-little-anymore guy was easily the station's worst-kept secret. Nobody cared about the new species of alien on their ship. Considering what the deckies saw on a daily basis, Zichix was not a big deal.

He had grown at an impressive rate lately. Chill thought it might have to do with where they were and what they were doing. However, they'd only met one other of his kind, so they were rare. She had found no studies to tell her what the norm for his species was.

All they could do was keep asking Zichix how he was feeling and judge whether he was healthy based on his answers.

"I guess that's the look I would have on *my* face if I just got back from blowing the shit out of a nest," Dorian greeted them, grinning. "Come on, guys. Beating the

Scourge back another step and living to talk about it is a win. I suggest we take it."

Chill patted the kid's shoulder. "Sure. It sucks that the whole Vert has to stay shut down until we figure out how to get those atmo and grav pockets working again, but you're right."

"Where was all that optimism when we were making our way back?" Ivan asked, climbing out of his armor. Their AI had walked Chill's and Kortez's armor back to the ship from where they'd left it. Ivan was more comfortable in his suit, so he'd kept his on.

"Yeah, she was silent and brooding the whole way back," Kortez chimed in.

"I wasn't. Well, I was silent, but I wasn't brooding. Just thinking. Considering the possibilities for the future, we can't throw all our efforts into just exploring this station. For one thing, at the rate we're going, it's going to take us the better part of a decade to get through the Verts, and that assumes the Scourge doesn't evolve in response and make it more difficult to keep pushing. As interesting as this place is, it's not going to work out well for us in the long run."

Dorian shrugged. "Seems a lot like brooding to me."

"It's thinking about a dark future." Chill scowled. "Doesn't mean I'm brooding. Now, unless any of you care to join me, I'm heading over to give our employer a status report."

"I'm fairly certain all four of us have more pressing engagements keeping us from joining you," Zichix commented, his eyes lining up to make it look like he was smiling. "But we wish you the best of luck."

Chill tried to maintain her scowl, but Zichix had a way of sapping the annoyance out of her. She couldn't stay mad at that face, or rather, his face equivalent.

"Right, I'm off." Her suit marched back into the ship, followed by the other riderless mechs. It had been their armorer's idea to have their AI run the empty suits, and it was ingenious. It allowed her to move them around without having to don them.

Everyone kept coming up with great ideas, and their operation was becoming more streamlined and efficient with each. She would let them get back to dealing with the repairs and restocking the ship.

Kuzratha had set up his operations in a tent in front of his ship. He was playing the part of the quirky and helpful provider of goods and bounties for the decky crews. It was working out well, as well as providing Coil Cove with a town center where they could purchase supplies, pick up work, and arrange to have a bounty split between multiple crews. A couple of vendors were selling food and drink to draw even more people to the new social center of their little base.

The Over-Keeper was dealing with the deckies who had salvage from the nest, although he didn't look happy about the quality of what was being delivered. In turn, the deckies weren't happy with the prices he offered them. Considering he was the only buyer, they had to take his offers. So far, he had been reasonable, so while they were complaining, they weren't making much of a fuss.

"Captain Chill." Kuzratha waved her over as he transferred creds to an interested party. "I understand that you have to keep your crew and mine and all others who go after the Scourge with you safe, but in the future, please try to avoid causing so much destruction."

"I'll keep it in mind." She crossed her arms. "In this case, we didn't have any choice since we had to vacate the area fast. Seems like taking on an active nest comes with dangerous repercussions. The node we were dealing with had defense mechanisms we hadn't accounted for. Also, up until this point, we hadn't appreciated that the Scourge is willing to allow the station to collapse to keep us from learning its secrets."

The Over-Keeper scratched his chin, then motioned for her to follow him into the back. Although they weren't dealing with people with the highest of morals in the galaxy, he trusted that the folks in Coil Cove didn't want to risk being cut from his cred supply—or get into a fight with the Janissaries who were guarding the area.

"I appreciate you coming to me with this information," Kuzratha continued as he closed the tent doors. He gestured for Chill to take a seat.

"Well, you *are* our employer, so it behooves me to keep you up to date on what we're doing." She took the offered seat, and he set up privacy countermeasures before doing the same. His chair matched the decor of the rest of the tent, making him look like a wandering peddler.

" I do appreciate the effort you've put into keeping the station intact. Of course, if the Scourge is willing to destroy Verts to defend itself, maybe destroying those Verts would not compromise the station as a whole. It does know more about the Serpent than we do, after all."

Chill nodded. "That is one possibility. Another is that it's willing to wreck the whole station if it means we keep our grubby mitts off its internal workings. Whatever the Scourge was when it was first developed, it now operates like a biological being rather than an AI, prone to—and I hate to say this—irrational behavior that might even lead to its own extinction. I'm not willing to threaten our endeavors on this station until we know more about how the Scourge will react to our presence."

"I see what you mean." He leaned back in his seat and his long, delicate fingers formed a triangle, which was something he did when he was lost in thought. Kortez and Ivan would probably think he was brooding, too. "Noted. For the moment, there is more important business for us to discuss."

"More important than running into the first AI in the galaxy to display biological thinking patterns?" Chill raised an eyebrow.

"While your suggestion has merit, Occami's Novaculum suggests that all we are facing here is a malfunctioning AI that does not comprehend that its actions are leading to its own demise."

"Occa... What?"

Kuzratha rolled his eyes. "Did you forget? The old Dahin theorem that says entities need not be multiplied beyond necessity, ergo, the simplest explanation is likely to be the correct one. Anyway, while discussing the state of the intelligence powering the Scourge is interesting, there are too many variables for it to be anything other than academic. I suggest we turn our minds to the new arrivals who came in today."

Chill leaned forward. "You're telling me that the first of the mercs are here?"

"You seem surprised."

"I assumed it would take them weeks or even months to gather the crew, materials, and weapons necessary to come to this dark and rather lonely point in space in hopes of getting the jump on a dangerous station."

"What can I say?" The Over-Keeper smiled. "The celebrity of the Dead Evil Mercenary Company has a magnetic pull on those looking to risk their lives for reward and adventure, enough to have them rushing in. They made port two hours ago, and we are taking security precautions to make sure they're not bringing any problems with them. We have too many issues as is to introduce new ones through negligence."

"A fair assumption," she answered. "How long have they been in those security checks?"

"They should be almost through, assuming they haven't brought any viral infections with them. They might already be out and about on the Serpent."

"Fun times. Do you think we should go meet them?"

"I think that would be best, considering the Dead Evil Mercenary Company was responsible for bringing them here. It would only be polite to introduce yourselves."

He was right. It would be polite to go and meet them in person. Chill wanted to make sure they knew what they were getting into. They could just be idiots looking to make a name for themselves, and she didn't want those deaths on her head. Kuzratha didn't seem to care.

"All right, let's get moving." She nodded for the Dahin to lead. She didn't trust him enough to turn her back on him. There was something unsettling about him. Kuzratha held the tent door open for her to step through.

Kuzratha had been right about greeting them. There was a commotion around the new ship. Not *new*, of course. It looked like an amalgam of several ships that had had a couple of decades of wear and tear on them before they were combined.

She also wasn't the first one to think about meeting the newcomers. Kortez and Ivan were there, likely having been drawn in by the novelty of the new ship in their hangar. Chill wasn't sure how she'd missed it. Being lost in thought and exhausted had clearly dulled her mental state, or maybe just her observational skills.

"Do you think there is a more popular member of your crew?" Kuzratha wondered aloud. tilting his head and watching the interactions of the new group with the pair. "I mean, the whole group is popular, from what I can see, but have you noticed a preference from the fans?"

"Have you ever watched our vids?" Chill countered.

"No. Just a couple of the highlight collections."

She nodded. "I guess you never went into the comment sections."

"No."

"Good. I advise you to avoid them." Chill shuddered. "Anyway, there are those who enjoy Ivan's skills and those who are interested in Zichix and his contributions. An unsettling number of them like me, although not because I am the most marketable face. There are quite a few of those. Avoid the comment sections unless you want graphic content. I suppose Kortez is the most popular in the group. There's something appealing about a big bastard who throws himself to the front of the battle."

"I suppose."

Chill started to feel like she didn't have the energy in her to deal with the newcomers. After a very long day, all she wanted was a quick shower, followed by a solid night's sleep before she had to make an appearance. She was not going to make good her escape, though.

Several people noticed her approaching and waved, then asked her to say a couple of words for their recordings. "Chill here," she began. "Been a rough go of it so far. We're damn glad to have the first wave of the cavalry here to help us. You guys are the..."

She turned to the one closest to her, a young man who was making a face at the cameras.

"We're the Star Hammers," he stated, nodding. "It's the bomb to meet a member of the Dead Evil Mercenary Company."

"You're going to be earning that 'bomb' in a bit," she answered, smiling at him. "It will be good to fight shoulder-to-shoulder with fellow mercs out here. I'm looking forward to more of you bolstering our ranks."

The ones around Kortez and Ivan were apparently interested in how Coil Cove had been set up. They were panning their cameras around as Ivan explained the station's setup and talked about the decky crews they would be working with.

It would be an interesting transition for everyone. Nothing was easy on the Serpent, although it looked like the newcomers were prepared. They were young, but they had armor and weapons similar to what she'd seen the independent crews on Mugh-9 use. The Star Hammers might have fought on the planet too, and she would have been surprised if they had crossed paths before.

Mugh-9 was a big planet, after all, and the DEMC had focused on the Dark Zone and its borders, where very few of the smaller crews ended up.

There was one element in their ensemble she didn't recognize. "What are those?" She pointed at the clubs hanging from their belts.

The man she'd talked to laughed and hefted the item. "We modeled ourselves after you. Not exactly, but close enough. We run a lean crew—five of us all told—and we thought we should have our own melee gimmick. Tried them out for the clicks, but it turns out they work."

Chill took a step back as he flicked his wrist to activate the weapon—a collapsible tac hammer. She had never seen the like.

"Star Hammers," she muttered, shaking her head. "That's... I like it."

"Really?"

"Yeah." She was surprised to find that she meant it. There was something about them—an enthusiasm she hadn't seen in a merc crew in a long time. It was a rough way to make a living. It ground people down and squeezed them out, turning even the most excited into cynics of the worst sort.

She wasn't arrogant enough to think she was above that, although she felt like she had come out better than most other mercs. They were either broken by the job, or a life of peace held no more appeal.

It was great to see folks who had clearly been through tough times yet still showed enthusiasm.

Kortez and Ivan clearly felt the same way. The former was eying the hammer with lust. Maybe she would have to pick one of those tactical hammers for him, something to go along with his new knife. He'd named the damn thing, but she couldn't remember what the name was for the life of her.

The Karen Cleaver. Karen Cortador? That was it, or something like that.

Not all of them had the same style of hammer. One of them had two that were heavier, clearly meant for cracking through Bugz chitin. They would likely be quite effective at crushing Scourge bots too. Another merc had batteries hooked up to his hammer, likely so it could act as a shock baton. The head of that hammer was lighter than the others.

The most interesting one was considerably longer than the others. It was meant to be handled like a polearm. The last one had more weight on the end and an inertial amplifier on the head, so it could flatten a tank if the merc put his mind to it.

That was the one Kortez wanted. She knew it almost before he did.

"Welcome, welcome, weary travelers." It appeared as though the Over-Keeper was tired of being ignored. He'd come out to greet them as well. "I am Kuzratha, a humble Dahin Wayfarer, looking to make his living alongside you in this place. If you have any need for supplies or direction on what kind of work would be the most profitable on the station, please come to my emporium. I am glad to help any and all who require my services."

A couple of the Hammers looked like they were interested in getting right to the work they had come to the Serpent to do. She didn't blame them. It was a long flight to the station, so they were rested and ready to crack skulls.

"I'm Blitz." One of them approached Chill, offering his hand. He was short and had a lean, athletic look. He looked a little older than the others, although she hadn't spotted it before because his tanned skin and dark hair made him look younger than he was. "A pleasure to be working with you, Captain Chill."

"I'm not the captain," she answered for what felt like the hundredth time as she shook his hand. "We run a democratic ship."

"Hey, we do the same thing, but...well, the rest of them look to me when they need level-headed guidance. That's not to say that *I'm* level, but compared to them, I am downright sane."

"I know the feeling." She smirked. "You'll need both crazy and calm to work out here. It's a hell of a balance. Anyway, I look forward to working with you and the rest of the Hammer crew, Blitz."

"And I you. I'd like to go over what will be expected from us around here. I'm sure you understand we're anxious to head into the thick of it with you."

"There isn't much in the way of sunshine and daisies around here." She thought it was important to temper their expectations from the start so they had a good idea of what they would be charging into. "It's a hell of a thing to share a station that's a couple of meters of steel away from the void of space with an AI that wants to kill you and has thousands of bots to carry its wishes out."

"Don't worry. We've followed your uploads on this

place. I had Scorch over there pick the vids apart to give us the details on the station before we arrived."

That was the sort of level-headed thinking they needed on the Serpent.

"With that in mind, you Hammers might want to stretch your legs and get the lay of the land." Chill motioned around the hangar. "Unfortunately, we just got back from a raid, so we need some rest and recovery time before we head out."

"Of course."

"I'll speak to you soon, Blitz. Welcome to Coil Cove."

She shook his hand again, and he headed off. Chill nodded for Kortez and Ivan to follow her back to their ship. They wanted to get to know their fans better, but food and sleep were important for their recovery. If they went into the field tired and distracted, it would get them killed.

They knew it too, but it was on her to make sure they remembered to care for themselves if they didn't do it on their own.

Maybe that *did* make her the captain, but she refused to take that title on.

The Over-Keeper approached her and spoke in a harsh whisper. "You think it was wise to tell them to wander around? They're fresh off the ship, and they'll want to get to work immediately. Why should we stop them from doing that?"

Chill scowled at the Jindahin but took the time to settle herself. No point in snapping at their employer.

"Remember the trouble we got into right after we arrived on the station?" she whispered back. "Give them a couple of hours to acclimate and get a feel for how we do things around here. That will help us when we're in the thick of a battle."

"There is still a lot of the Serpent for you to...liberate before we can start on the next stage of our work." He looked around to make sure nobody was eavesdropping on them before continuing. "Before we can stabilize the wormhole, we will need to control a great deal more of the station."

"Stabilize the wormhole?"

"Why do you think we didn't just jump through the wormhole into the nebula?" He tilted his head. "We have to stabilize it before it's safe to use it, and that requires we take a lot more of the station. Having the newcomers work in tandem with you and your crew is not the most efficient way to clear the Serpent."

Chill halted as her temper rose and turned to the Dahin. "First, there is no 'we,'" she hissed. "You are providing support, but we're the ones heading in there. You owe it to us to trust our instincts on the best and most efficient way of doing this."

He was taken aback that Chill spoke to him in that manner. His mouth opened and closed, but she didn't give him the opportunity to regain his composure.

"Secondly, I won't throw them into the teeth of the Scourge just because you want the new arrivals to go to work as soon as they land." She looked at the Hammers, who were exploring Coil Cove, although Blitz was watching her conversation with the "Wayfarer." "Throwing newcomers into a fight with the Scourge is a good way to get them killed, and if word gets around that people are being massacred, more won't come."

Chill couldn't help but feel that the Over-Keeper knew that and there was another reason he was so keen for them to move faster but wrote it off as annoyance and paranoia.

Given how close things had been in the nest raid, she felt their slow progress was justified. They had to make sure their efforts weren't wasted, or worse, stretched themselves too far, too quickly.

She didn't know if the Scourge knew tactics, but if it did, waiting for them to stretch their resources to the breaking point would be brilliant.

Kortez assumed the AI was still operating on its original protocols. After they depleted the majority of its resources, it would shut down and hide in the station's programs until it had a good opportunity to strike.

They could get smashed in a Scourge counterattack if it brought enough numbers to bear.

Kuzratha likely knew that too, which explained why he took a deep breath to calm himself and then nodded. "I suppose you are right. I brought you in to handle the situation, and I'll have to trust your judgment."

Chill couldn't tell if he meant the non-apology, but she didn't have the time to pick his words apart. "If you'll follow me, it would be better if we debriefed you on the operation on our ship." Chill indicated for him to follow her. "We'll need privacy."

Kuzratha followed her. Dorian was waiting for them with a tablet in hand. He wasn't sure what the Over-Keeper was doing there.

"Dorian," Chill greeted him with a smile. "How's your day been?"

"Work never stops," he answered, still trying to figure out why the Jindahin was with her. He shrugged. "We should go over what I managed to pick up from the nest, even if my access was cut short."

"The countervirus worked as expected, then?" Kuzratha interjected, taking a step closer.

Dorian narrowed his eyes, then shook his head. "Not as expected, no. That code was written hundreds of years before the countervirus was even a twinkle in its creator's eye, so I had to do a significant amount of real-time fiddling to make it even halfway effective. That was most of what I was doing while we were connected, so we'll need to connect it to another nest to see if my alterations were worth our time. Still, I *was* able to mine some data about the Scourge's core code."

Dorian handed the fob with the data to the Over-Keeper, who plugged it into his tablet and scanned the contents.

The Jindahin's stoic expression changed. "You think you could collect more if you found another nest?" Kuzratha asked, still looking at the data.

"Without a doubt," Dorian asserted with more confidence than he'd displayed during the raid. "The Scourge might adapt, but most of the hard work is done. It'll be a lot more effective the next time around."

"Interesting."

Chill cleared her throat. She didn't disagree—although she did want to double-check the kid's work—but she wanted to keep the conversation moving forward.

"Whatever data Dorian mined justifies our venture into the nest, which doesn't count the tons of salvage the deckies will recover from the wreckage over the coming days. Of course, their work would move a lot faster if they didn't have to worry about grav and atmo problems."

The Dahin looked up from his tablet. "You think this effort amounts to the kind of success I pay you for?"

"I know it does, and you do too. Besides, we're going to have to start spreading creds around to the people who aren't salvaging if we want them to repair the station as we break it. They shouldn't focus on salvage as the only profitable enterprise on the station."

She expected more hemming and hawing over her request. Negotiation was his second language, after all, yet he pulled a bunch of creds out of a pocket, put them in a pouch, and handed them to her.

"Your progress *is* impressive, Captain Chill." He stepped half a meter closer to her than Chill was comfortable with. "I expect you to keep producing impressive results."

"Just Chill, not captain." She forced a smile. " You'll just have to wait and see."

Antagonizing their employer wasn't a bright move, but she couldn't help it. If he pushed them to conform to an agenda he was keeping from them, she would push back.

She'd hoped he'd learned they didn't need to be micromanaged, but he was getting more annoying.

After the Jindahin left, she waited until he was out of earshot before pulling out the cred chits, dividing them, and handing the majority to Dorian.

"What—"

"Shoviil is waiting outside." She answered his question

before he asked it. "Give these to him and tell him to get the repair crews on the Vert."

"Will do."

He tipped an imaginary cap at her as Chill shook her head. They had to divvy up the creds she still had, but she wasn't in the mood for it. Something to eat, a shower to get rid of the mech smell, and a nap would do the trick.

CHAPTER FOUR

Chill was calmer after she ate and got some sleep.

There was no shaking the stress that came from living on the Serpent. She didn't know how people could do it long-term. Living on a station, one mistake away from being sucked out into the void, was hard enough, but there was also a malicious presence here that wanted to kill her and everyone else.

Chill had heard about sub-sonic waves, which, with continued exposure, made the person who was subjected to them paranoid and angry. They even started seeing things out of the corners of their eyes.

She'd read about them on the caster networks, so the information had to be taken with a heaping pile of salt, but here on the station, she believed it was possible.

"Are you brooding again?"

Zichix had joined her, approaching cautiously.

"I'm not—" She stopped herself. They would use the word as long as it annoyed her, so she had to get used to it. "Just lost in thought. Considering the possibility that we are being affected by sub-sonic waves that could be making us all paranoid and irritable. Or maybe it's just me. Maybe a couple of sleep enhancers would do the trick."

"Well, to set your suspicions to rest, if any sub-sonic waves were being emitted on the station, I could detect them. There are vibrations from the wormhole generators, but the waves they emit are harmless." Zichix leaned closer and studied her. "I sense that didn't help the way I hoped it would."

"No, no. It's good to know there's nothing acting on my brain from the outside," Chill admitted.

"But you're worried about the implications." He started preparing food for himself with his forelimbs. "Most importantly, if your paranoia is not caused by an external force, it might be a more commonplace and yet equally distressing mental health issue."

"Something like that, yeah."

"I see." He returned his attention to food prep since he needed both eyes and two of his limbs to handle the knife. It was equal parts cute and fascinating to watch him carefully and yet deftly handle a tool that was not designed with a creature like him in mind. "Unfortunately, my knowledge of human psychology is lacking. I did find a handful of starter texts, but they were dull. I was distracted by the different mineral densities of planets that have been terraformed and the implications for the sentient life that settles on those planets."

"That's fair. I couldn't get too deep into the subject either." Chill wasn't going to tell him she found mineral density just as tedious. "I could download programs and apps to get me started on therapy. Even if they fail to work, they would still diagnose my mental state based on an algorithm and recommend a therapist. Might as well look into it."

"Look into what?" Dorian interjected as he stepped into the mess.

"Oh, I was just paying out bonuses to your individual accounts," Chill shot back, flicking her tablet off. "I was explaining to Zichix that I'm going to be transferring a double amount to Kortez because there's no account in his own name. We're not sure how to get him registered so a bank would let him open one. Might take a little while."

"That's not true," Zichix corrected. "Chill was just telling me that she is feeling an unusual amount of paranoia and distress that started with her arrival on Suneater Station. We were discussing whether there was an external cause or if it was possibly indicative of a mental health issu—"

Chill coughed, shook her head, and swiped her hand across her throat to cut the little guy off before he could continue.

"I now realize that Chill confided in me under the assumption that I would keep her confidence," Zichix surmised, doing his version of frowning. "I'm sorry."

"No problem."

"Wait." Dorian shook his head. "Are you saying she *didn't* transfer the creds to our accounts yet?"

"No, I transferred everyone's creds," Chill answered. "Before the conversation about my possible mental deterioration."

"Hold on." Zichix turned back around. "So, you really *aren't* sure how to register me as a sentient with the proper authorities."

"Well, for starters, we don't know which authorities to register you with." Chill rubbed her temples. "Kortez and I agreed you would get the same pay as the rest of the crew, and it would be transferred into his account to be transferred to yours when we get around to opening it. Deducting living expenses, of course. I have the record of what I've paid you, and he said he's doing the same with the expenses you've incurred, so nobody will cheat you out of your earnings. You could also hire an attorney to help you register. I can cover the expense out of the ship's budget until we get you situated."

Zichix considered the possibility but shook his eyes from side to side the way a human would have shaken their head. "I don't think that'll be necessary. I trust my dad."

"Like I said, it's your decision."

"Can we go back to Chill going crazy?" Dorian asked, raising his hand.

"We cannot," she growled. "What's on your mind, Dorian?"

"On that topic," Zichix offered, ignoring her, "I have been keeping track of the crew's health states since we arrived on Suneater, and I've picked up elevated stress levels across the board. I don't have anything to compare your current states to aside from the yearly medical checks Dad, Ivan, and Chill were required to take while they were employed as mercenaries on Mugh-9, which were far from sufficient. Several steps need to be taken. For instance, Dad's red meat intake needs to be assessed, considering that his arterial health is a far cry from what it was three years ago."

"You're going to tell Kortez to eat less red meat?" Dorian raised an eyebrow. "Can I be there when you do?"

"I was hoping to discuss his colonic health as well. Do you have the medical background required to go over those details with me?"

"No, but I'd really like to see you tell him he can't eat red meat."

Zichix straightened. "I'm sorry, but I take my role as the ship's medical officer seriously, and while I might have made a mistake by sharing intimate details about Chill's mental state, I will not do so again."

Chill scratched her chin. "You might have, you know, discussed Kortez's health with us too."

"Oh." The insectoid shook his eyestalks again. "Crap."

"What did I tell you about language?" Kortez interjected as he joined them in the mess hall. "Come on! I don't want other people to think I'm raising you entirely without principles."

"You use that kind of language all the time," Zichix pointed out.

"I was raised entirely without principles. What were you guys talking about?"

"Zichix was telling us that you're going to have to cut down on red meat," Dorian stated with a grin. "There might be something wrong with your colon too, but he didn't go into details."

"What?" Kortez snapped.

"There's no need to be embarrassed, Dad," Zichix assured him. "I gestated inside you. There's no reason to be bashful."

"Oh, yeah, it's every father's dream to talk about his diet with his kid." Kortez sighed, shaking his head.

"Here I was, expecting there to be more pushback on him telling you that you need to eat less red meat," Dorian muttered. He took a bite of the sandwich he'd made.

"Oh, there will be," Kortez grumbled. "There is every time he suggests he poke and prod me in the name of my health."

"I expected there would be as well." Zichix finished making his meal. He apparently did not care that the flash-frozen fish was still raw as he started eating. "And I expect pushback from all of you, even though my suggestions will benefit your health and are therefore in line with your evolutionary drive for continued survival. It is fascinating that humans are so averse to maintaining their health."

"We can't help it," Chill muttered. "We've been dealing with that since the dawn of time. We don't like being poked and prodded by people who are smarter than we are."

"Indeed. I also expect there to be pushback when I tell Chill she requires a handful of procedures, including a mammogram, so I can continue to monitor her health. Her opening up about her possible mental health issues has me thinking I am on the right track, though."

Chill glared at Zichix as he tossed food into his mouth. "That's a talk for another time."

If Zichix was taking the job of ship's medical officer seriously, she would comply with his requests—within reason. They would have to have a long and detailed conversation regarding medical confidentiality, but he would eventually get it.

She had to admit the awkward conversation about the

medical exams they all needed to undergo was a distraction from how she was feeling. Zichix was saying that Ivan needed to undergo a series of tests to determine if being around explosives had had any effects on him. Chill smirked.

"I don't want to know how he's going to look at Ivan's insides since I'm sure it will be gross, so if I could change the subject?" Dorian interrupted. "I'd like to discuss our financial situation. I've taken stock of our equipment and funds over the past few days, and while we've taken in a steady financial stream from the loot we've brought back as well as the payments we've gotten from the Over-Keeper and our investments, we're not going to be making any big career moves. Even with the revenue coming in from our caster channel, we're just managing to stay afloat."

"It's to be expected," Chill pointed out. "Kuzratha is only covering our expenses while we clear the station. It's stipulated in our contract that our big payday comes after the Serpent has been cleared. There will also be a completion bonus, which will amount to a fortune. As long as we stick to the grind of clearing the station, we'll come out well ahead. Assuming, of course, we all make it. If we don't, I imagine Dorian, Ibu, and Zichix will get the fuck out of here and split up the creds from our savings accounts and the sale of the ship."

Zichix let out a sound Chill assumed was a scoff. "I wouldn't leave my dad behind."

"That's my boy." Kortez bumped his fist into one of the insectoid's appendages. "We shouldn't be thinking about that. We just got paid, so I say that we head out to celebrate. Did you see that one of the deckies set a little pub up outside Kuzratha's place? We should inspect it before the rest of the merc crews show up to make sure it's up to the standard they will be expecting."

"I doubt anything on the station will meet standard health and safety codes," Zichix pointed out.

"Not what I was talking about. Come on. We need some time out of the ship. I'll get Ivan and Ibu. Then we can go over there and see how the place is."

"Just don't talk to Ivan about what Zichix plans on doing to him," Dorian pointed out. "I have a feeling that'd put him off drinking."

"Probably a good idea," Chill agreed. "Let's go."

Dorian tilted his head. "Wait, is drinking the good idea, or not telling Ivan?"

"Yes. Come on."

They were much too sober to discuss their medical conditions. After they were good and plastered so nobody would remember anything, they could overshare.

They weren't the first to think of going out drinking. It was the night cycle on the station, which meant work was done for the day. Most of the crews had just gotten substantial paychecks for salvaging what remained of the nest. Not as much as they'd hoped they would get, but enough to justify copious drinking and celebrating.

They'd cleared a nest. It wasn't the big victory they had been hoping for, but it was still a victory. It was good to celebrate their wins, even if they hadn't come out the way she wanted them to.

She smiled when all the drinkers raised their mugs to the DEMC as they approached the pub. It had been put together in a haphazard fashion, but it would do. She had no idea where they were getting their beer, but they'd been on the station for decades with very little interaction with the outside world, so they had found ways to sustain themselves. It looked and smelled right, and they served it ice-cold to the point where frost formed on the sides of the mugs.

"A round for the group," Chill called to one of the three bartenders. "And a round for everyone else. To a job well-fucking-done!"

It got a cheer out of the deckies, as she'd expected it would. They could afford to throw their creds around since the drinks were surprisingly cheap, and they needed to keep the morale of the crews up. What they were doing wasn't easy, and if she wanted them to stay on her side, she had to keep them happy as well as employed.

Nothing got to a merc's heart faster than free drinks. She'd learned that a long time ago when it was someone else buying her the drinks.

They took one of the few free tables, and six mugs were banged down on it. Chill didn't think Zichix was old enough to drink, but it wasn't her decision to make. Despite his initial doubts and protests, Kortez was parenting the little alien, so she would respect whatever decision he made.

Within reason.

Chill raised her mug. "To wrecking another nest. May there be many more to come!"

Ambiguous though her wording was, the rest of the crew raised their mugs as well, although Zichix had to use three of his limbs to lift his.

"Hear, hear," Kortez growled. Then he took a swig of his drink.

"Well-said, boss," Ibu added with a grin, taking a sip of hers.

Nothing more was said until their mugs were at least half-empty. Kortez had downed most of his, so the rules dictated he had to pick up the next round.

"Of all the places to find ourselves drinking," Ivan whispered, shaking his head. "A station that creates a wormhole that's orbited by three dwarf stars has to be the nuttiest place I've ever been."

"Agreed." Chill nodded. "I never imagined things going this way, but I wouldn't want to do this with anyone else. Well, maybe not Dorian."

"Fuck you, boss." The kid grinned and took another swig from his mug. "I would never have thought I would end up in a place like this either. There comes a time, though, when you have to take your situation by the balls and squeeze it for all it's worth."

"Maybe a less horrifying metaphor," Ivan suggested. "Besides, your path to joining the DEMC was stealing Zichix and running away after we put ourselves on the line to save your life from the people you'd pissed off on the station."

"He makes a solid point," Chill agreed. "This is about as good a situation as you could have ended up in."

Before Chill could chide him on his language in front of Zichix, they heard a commotion from the entrance to the pub.

"Sounds like a fight." Kortez sounded excited by the possibility. He pushed halfway out of his seat to see where it was coming from. "Looks like a fight too. Beginnings of one, anyway."

Chill turned around to see what all the shouting was about, and Kortez was right. The Hammers were shouting insults at one of the decky crews, which had gotten the attention of the other crews. They either wanted to watch or thought they were being insulted too.

"Shit," she muttered. "And here I was, hoping for a quiet celebratory drink."

"Fuck that." The big guy got to his feet. "Been a while since I was in a proper brawl. Too long."

"Remember, it has to look like you're trying to stop the fight before it breaks out," Chill reminded him.

There was never a dull moment. Chill got up, leaving her weapons behind. Brawls were fine, but when someone pulled a caster out, she would put a stop to it.

CHAPTER FIVE

Where had her life gone? It hadn't been *that* long since she'd joined fights without asking why they were taking place. It was a good way to let off steam.

Now here she was, trying to stop this one before it escalated. How pathetic was that?

She had to be a responsible leader. If she wasn't, they would die on the station. Chill had no idea how she had become the adult, but she was going to assume it was only relevant to their current situation. When she didn't have the responsibility for an entire station and those who lived on it hanging over her, she would join the fun without a second thought.

Until then, this shit had to stop.

"All right, that's enough!" she snapped and grabbed one of the Hammers before he could throw the punch he had lined up.

No one heard her. She stepped in to stop one of the deckies from taking advantage of the Hammer's distraction. If she started throwing punches, the rest of them would join in. Since that was the opposite of her intention, Chill had to keep the two parties from fighting without resorting to violence.

"The next person who throws a punch gets me in their face instead!" Kortez roared.

Chill could have told him that would just get the fight going, but before she could interject, someone did it for her—one of the deckies. He was short, stocky, and looked like he could trace his ancestry to several hominid species. He tried to get around Kortez to attack one of the Hammers who had flung an insult regarding his mother.

Kortez proved his way of playing it was the correct one. He grabbed the attacker by the throat and smoothly flipped him over his hip, and the decky landed on the floor with a thud and a grunt. The display was enough to grab the attention of the others, stunning them into a hushed silence as Kortez towered over the wheezing decky.

"I fucking warned him," the larger man growled, eying the rest to see who else needed a physical warning.

No one stepped forward. Maybe, in this case, violence did not beget violence, although Chill doubted she could pull that sort of thing off. She was capable of holding her own, but when her opponents registered her size and weight, they usually took their chances. With Kortez, who was ten or twenty centimeters taller than the rest, the fighters had to consider the costs and benefits of tangling with him.

Assuming they were sober enough to think that far ahead, of course, but once they got to thinking, their will to throw fists went away.

The DEMC had good reason to side with the deckies in

a fight. Their relationship with the crews was established, and they knew how effective the decky crews were, whereas the Hammers were unknowns.

That said, it didn't bode well for their future relationship with the other mercenary crews if they engaged in violence with them the moment they arrived.

At least in the first twenty-four hours. She had a feeling it would happen at some point, but right now, it was on her to keep the aggressiveness from turning into an outright war.

"Anyone else feeling like talking with their fists?" Chill asked, looking each of them in the eye until they looked away. "You think the Scourge is out there thinning its own ranks for our benefit? Fighting between us is going to lead to a lot more people dying. Division will kill us as quickly as any rogue AI bot.

"Well, faster if you piss Kortez off. Get your shit together!"

"They're the ones invading our space!" one of the deckies shouted, the one she'd stopped. "They will come in and take over and push us out one crew at a time. We're just putting a stop to it before they can do that."

"Bullshit," Blitz snapped. "You were showing us that the new arrivals would be treated like second-class citizens, and we fought back!"

"Enough!" This time, they listened to her. Chill took a deep breath, trying to keep from losing her temper. If she was going to be the voice of reason, she had to tap into whatever they saw in her that made them think she was leadership material. "If you're going to fight over castes, you might go to a Vert and let the Scourge spare you the trouble. If you want to remain in Coil Cove, we all have to stand together."

That was a repeat of what she'd told the deckies the first time they'd run into each other, which was frustrating.

The decky shook his head. "How are—"

"No. You think you can fight the Scourge off alone and keep it off in the spots you do take back? Hell, can you populate the station enough to make it even barely functional?" Chill shook her head. "We're going to need every able body out there to win this, nothing less.

"Yes, there are more merc crews on the way. That means we'll have more people to fight on our side when the going gets tough. It means we'll be able to push out further and diminish the Scourge that much more. More resources, more weapons, a better setup. Is this the way you want to start out? Bickering about who is higher on the social ladder?"

It seemed like she was making her point. Chill hadn't thought about any of that before, but when she started talking, everyone else shut up and listened.

What she was saying made sense. It was a big station, and they were only occupying a miniscule percentage of it. If they intended to make it functional, they would need a lot more people.

If Kuzratha wanted to bring his folks in to take over, that was his call. For the moment, he was trusting her to make the right choices to further their plan as discussed.

"Anyone have anything to add?" she asked when the silence wore on longer than she was comfortable with. "I'm all for throwing fists over insults to one's parentage. However, if you're going to fight, make it for the right reasons. Once it's done, brush yourselves off, shake hands, and buy each other drinks to make up for the bruising. If that's not what you had in mind, back the fuck off."

The fight had left all of them. Chill wondered if she was better at pep talks than she'd thought. As long as what they did wouldn't make fighting the Scourge more difficult, she was okay with their decisions, although there were limits.

They shuffled off with their crews and talked about their situation. Chill wondered how long it would take until they provoked each other again. As long as they did it within the parameters she'd outlined, she was fine with that. Mercenaries who spent their lives killing others for money were expected to get into barfights. Throwing punches and taking their frustrations out on each other was fine as long as it ended in or around the bar and they didn't take the fights out to the field.

In the past, Chill had seen people turn on their own people in the heat of battle. They were the lowest of the low as far as she was concerned. There were plenty of ways for them to work out their frustrations safely back at the base.

"So, you yelling at them got them in line," Ivan commented. "We could always crack a few skulls to remind them of the bigger problems on the Serpent."

"Except *I'm* the one cracking the skulls." Kortez scowled. "Why is it always me?"

"You're not really complaining," Chill answered. She nodded for them to head back to their table. "You always get out of it just fine. Besides, everyone seems to listen to you when they're on the verge of throwing down."

"It's not my fault that they end up thinking twice about

pairing off with me." Kortez shrugged. "But yeah, you're right. I needed to throw someone around. You just don't get the same feeling when you're fighting bots. Or Bugz, for that matter."

Chill smirked. "You telling me you had more fun in our little war against the Dahins than you did when we were clearing Bugz out?"

"Not really. I mean, there's a disconnect when you're fighting Bugz and bots. Not anymore, of course. Not with the Bugz, anyway. Knowing they're a sentient species makes you realize... I don't know."

She didn't know either, but she understood what he was talking about. It wasn't a pleasant realization, but it was their reality. Either they would grow numb to it, or it would break them.

"Don't know about any of you, but I'm not in the mood to eat or drink here anymore," Chill whispered as the food she'd ordered was placed on the table. Serving food and drink wasn't a career in Coil Cove, but the owner of the place was making do. It was a decent way for those who had the time to make creds.

Chill didn't have much left over, but she handed a couple of cred chits to the server.

"But you—"

She nodded. "That's to cover the damage."

A couple of tables and chairs had been broken. They had been put together from salvage, so it wasn't a huge setback, but it would piss people off if they weren't paid for their labor. They weren't going to stick around for the rest of the evening's entertainment. Chill packed up her food, and the others did as well. They would enjoy their down-time on the ship, as had been the original plan.

"I...thank you." The server was young and second- or third-generation decky if she had to guess. One of the humans who had explored the area and settled on the station for whatever reason.

There were no records left from that far back, and the station's hard storage units had long since stopped recording. The details of how the various decky crews had come to be on the station were lost, and those that remained had been heavily warped by being passed down by word of mouth.

An anthropological study might fill in the historical details, but she doubted any would focus on what had happened on the station in the future. In fact, her guess was that the Jindahin who would run the station in the future would cover everything up, hide the truth, and make sure nobody questioned why the station was shut down for so long.

It would be one hell of a job. Hundreds of thousands of PR agents would flood the area to spin the tale of how they'd taken the station back in a way that made the Jindahin look good. Chill knew that half the history texts were written by PR people to make someone look good or bad. It was just a matter of finding out who had done the writing and where their budget had come from.

That was a matter for later. Chill narrowed her eyes as Blitz approached her with the rest of his people in tow. "I appreciate you interceding on our behalf, captain," he began. "I don't know what would have happened if you hadn't shown up."

"I do," Kortez muttered. "Lots of people would have gotten hurt for no damn good reason."

"Is that your commentary on brawls?" Dorian asked, raising an eyebrow. "Doesn't seem like the sharpest take on the matter."

"Brawls happen for a good reason," the bigger man snarled. "Getting into it with friends and comrades over a pint is always worth your while. Picking a fight with someone you barely know? That's a waste."

"Anyway," Chill interrupted, glaring at Kortez, "it would have been an awful way to start you off on the station. Still, you're going to have to take it easy with the deckies. They have a lot of pride in who they are, and having newcomers come into their territory is a new idea for them."

Blitz nodded. "I had a feeling that was their problem with us."

"Should have seen how they reacted when *we* showed up," Dorian muttered. "Sent us off to fight the Scourge, then tried to take our ship, our people, and our mechs. Didn't help them much, considering how many other people they'd pissed off, but, well, there's a scavenging culture around here. If you can get your hands on it, it's yours."

That didn't improve the Hammers' opinion of the locals, but Chill wasn't going to put much effort into that. They didn't have to like each other as long as they got along.

"I suppose there's nothing for it," Blitz answered, joining them on their walk back to their ship. "It doesn't help that the Hammers have had to fight their way through just about every situation they've been in. They are a scrappy bunch, sometimes finding fights where none should have happened."

"You talk like you're not one of them."

"I...huh. Never noticed that. Nothing personal in it, but since I'm older, I've always been...apart in some way, I guess. Anyway, we've mostly been on the small-time side of merc work, usually escort and security gigs. Spent a bit of time in the fighting between the Dominion and Enterprise frontier forces. That was mostly urban guerilla warfare, building weapons and traps out of whatever we could get our hands on. That's where our liking of those hammers came from."

"Funny how that worked out," Kortez interjected. "I don't suppose you know where one might get his hands on one of those hammers? Asking for a friend."

"Not now," Chill whispered. "Besides, can't you look on the caster net? There are plenty of delivery systems that could send Kuzratha whatever you buy."

"You never know what you're going to get when you order over the nets." Kortez shook his head. "In the end, I'd have to pick it up off of a military surplus site, and they'd end up overcharging for a product whose quality was too poor to send to the front line for their own troops."

He had a point. Military surplus was always a gamble and one that very few people won

"We picked them up from local sellers on the ground," Blitz answered helpfully. "Not as they are now, of course. We put time and effort into adapting them for our own styles of combat. Field testing was required as well."

"I guess you'll just have to find a hammer of your own and adapt it to your style of fighting." Chill patted the big man on the back in what she hoped was a comforting manner.

"Wait, he was asking for himself, not a friend?" Blitz tilted his head, looking confused.

"I…yes, it's for me." Kortez shook his head. "I've been wielding my Cortador for a while, but I feel like it's time for her to pick up a comrade for the field of battle."

"How would your knife find herself a comrade?"

It was Chill's turn to be confused. She studied Blitz to determine if he was joking or genuinely having trouble understanding what they were talking about.

She had a flash of insight. "You're from Habbershad, aren't you?"

"Yes." Blitz grinned. "That is amazing. I thought I'd done away with my Shaddie accent."

"It's a gift." Chill smiled. She'd only run into a couple of Shaddies, but their cultural oddities made them stand out in her mind. "What brought you from selling your services on border planets all the fucking way out here?"

"A fair question, I suppose." He turned to the rest of the Hammers, who were right behind him, but none of them said anything. They were staring and smiling like they couldn't believe they were on Serpent. "We were taking jobs from the frontier forces, mostly side work nobody else could be bothered with. Got some work protecting a small community caught in the middle of the fighting. It was steady and ensured we didn't have to wait around for one of the military sides to decide they needed us to escort a supply run. Besides, it's the good kind of work, keeping regular folk safe instead of protecting the interests of some corporate nozzle halfway across the galaxy."

It was the preferred kind of work. Chill agreed with him, although it wasn't always a possibility. Violent careers were generally associated with greedy rich assholes who took their frustrations out on other greedy rich assholes. However, occasionally, mercs found work that allowed them to have a functional soul as well as a stable income.

That was how she felt about the work they'd done for the Bugz, although it had ended up putting them on course for a fiery end to their relationship with the Perdahin and, therefore, the Kahdahin. She would not feel comfortable going back to that region of space for a while. She'd likely have to wait until the two denominations started fighting over Mugh-9 again.

Blitz shook his head. He'd been talking while she'd been lost in thought, and apparently, she'd missed a humorous anecdote about their time with the local civilian community.

"Anyway, it made us feel like there was more to our kind of life than attacking whatever target the bosses said was a threat to their endeavors. We ended up being more selective about the kind of work we picked up. We all agreed on it. Had a meeting and everything. Some infighting, but in the end, our cred reserves allowed us to be pickier. Instead of holding out for the better-paying jobs, we decided on the ones that didn't make us feel like shit before, during, and after."

"That makes sense." Chill nodded as the party came to a halt by their ship. "Not everything's going to work out the way you want it to. Not saying everyone can, but most of those who *can* pick the decent jobs end up choosing the work that pays more."

She would be the first to admit that working with Kuzratha felt slimy.

"Anyway, that's what brought us here." Blitz turned to the rest of the Hammers, who nodded. "It seemed like we could work for ourselves instead of serving some corp's interest. You and your team did state that it was a tough place to make a living, so maybe the competition won't be quite so thick."

"Not really." Chill shrugged. "Our hope is that plenty of other mercs will find their way out here. I'm interested in how much work you can find on this station. I assume you saw just how large the station is on your way in?"

He nodded.

"Well, Coil Cove is the only part of the station that is free of hostiles. We haven't been able to push farther out than this Vert—that is what they call the individual sections—because we don't want to overextend ourselves. Each is inhabited by dangerous bots that will be worth their weight in cadmium to the right buyer. Those, as it turns out, are the other decky crews and Kuzratha, although he will pay a little more if you bring in certain items he's looking for. Processors, motherboards, that kind of thing."

Blitz tilted his head. "Is that the only kind of work we'll be doing while we're here?"

"No, that's the reward for your other work." Chill knew they had potential but sending them straight into the jaws of the Scourge seemed like a poor way to greet their first arrivals. "It would be best if you go on a couple of our raids into Scourge territory. Give yourselves an idea of the kind of shit you'll face out there."

"You don't trust us to go out there on our own?" another of the Hammers asked. Considering that her short hair had been dyed bright red and yellow, she assumed the woman was Scorch. "I mean, we've been in combat before."

"We trust your combat skills," Kortez interjected before Chill could. "But I'm pretty sure the Scourge will catch anyone by surprise the first time. Fuck, we're still running into shit we've never seen before and hope never to see again. It's a good idea to have backup out there, just in case."

Chill nodded her agreement. "You and the other merc crews are going to be an integral part of our efforts to get rid of the Scourge and get this station back into working order. You'll also have plenty of opportunities to bring salvage back to be sold."

"What if we're all busy killing this Scourge and the other crews clean out all the salvageable materials?" Blitz asked.

"We've had this discussion with the decky crews. The income from the salvage will be divided between those involved in recovering it and those who turn it into something that can be sold. It's a complex system, but our AI is keeping track of what's brought in as well as the funding to make sure that the creds are divided properly when the funds roll in. And no, neither I nor any of my crew has any contact with the pool account. As soon as the creds are paid into it, they are in turn paid out. All crews have full viewing privileges for the account to ensure full transparency. It's actually a good system. Dorian here came up with it."

Dorian's eyes widened when their attention turned to him. "No need to point. They know who I am."

She continued, "There is room for individuals to earn, which is where Kuzratha and the other crews come in. if you find something you can carry on your own, you can sell it to our Dahin Wayfarer or someone else, provided they're willing to pay for it. Doesn't need to be what you pick up from the fallen bots. It can be equipment someone left behind. They abandoned it decades or centuries ago, so if nothing else, they will be antiques. Just don't get too greedy, and nobody will mind. Like I said before, there's plenty of salvage to go around on this station."

That was how she'd presented the idea to the rest of the crews, verbatim. They had been uncertain and suspicious, but after a few weeks using the system had proven everyone was getting paid the proper amounts, and they were all happy. Or at least, they didn't have a basis to complain.

Yet. Problems would arise, of that she was certain.

Blitz had followed her explanation, but Chill could tell that he still had a few questions. "I've always been confused. In your vids, you talk about the Scourge being a viral attack, but you also refer to it like it's a living entity."

"I guess we do." Chill tilted her head. "They're not like anything we've seen before. We know they're bots run on a network, which does indicate artificial intelligence, but there's more to it than that, or I think there is. I'm sure the experts out there will say I'm anthropomorphizing the intelligence, which I've heard is common."

"I see."

She sighed. "Well, this is where we get off. The station

runs on a day and night cycle, so it shouldn't be difficult to keep track of the time. What do you say we all rest up and meet here tomorrow at oh-seven hundred hours sharp?"

"That would be fantastic." Blitz grinned, and all the other Hammers did as well. "See you soon, Captain."

"Right, and I'm…not the captain." Chill shook her head, knowing her protests were falling on deaf ears. The other mercs headed toward their ship after saying their goodnights.

"She's actually letting a few of them go," Dorian commented. "People call her captain all the time, and she only corrects them, like, twenty-five percent of the time. Could it be that Chill is warming to the title everyone keeps giving her?"

"She is not," Chill muttered, shaking her head. "I don't suppose anyone around here understands there's such a thing as a captainless ship?"

"I don't think they care," Ibu responded to the rhetorical question. "The apparent leader of a crewed ship is perceived as the captain regardless of how the captain perceives herself. Of course, it falls on the captain to come up with something other than a generic name for her ship."

"It's… I'm getting around to that." Chill scowled. She wasn't in the mood for this. Her nap hadn't gotten her rested up enough for it. "You know how hard it is to name a ship? Ships have a whole fucking personality, and if I get the name wrong, it'll be on the records and make my eyes ache every time I see it."

"We do understand the difficulties." Kortez wrapped his arm around her shoulders. "That's why we're leaving the job to you. Make it happen, Cap…ow!"

Elbowing him in the ribs proved to be more effective than correcting him for calling her captain. It didn't matter, though; people would keep doing it. Chill just didn't want to accept it because by doing so, she would have to assume the responsibilities permanently.

"Just get some rest and be ready to move out." Ordering people about did have a certain appeal.

Dorian offered a mock salute. "Aye aye—"

"Don't." She pointed a finger at him. "Just...don't."

A good night's sleep did help. Chill still wasn't in the finest of moods, but she was coming to terms with the Dead Evil crew pestering her about the leadership situation. They knew it was a weak point, and like voracious raptors, they would pounce on it for every scrap of flesh they could get.

All she could do was sigh, roll her eyes, and let them get their hits in. It was easier since she knew she would do the same thing in their position.

With the nap she'd taken before, she was up and ready ahead of the rest of the crew, although Ibu wasn't far behind. The woman never looked tired. She was always the same steady, reliable armorer they needed on their team. She was always up and ready at the crack of dawn to make sure the suits were ready for deployment.

"These things are built like fucking tanks, you know?" Ibu commented as Chill cleaned out the inside of hers.

"I assumed tanks had a lot more armor on them," she answered, not looking up from her work. Maybe with a little more elbow grease, she wouldn't have to smell her own stale sweat for hours on end. "Even the lighter anti-grav ones."

"They do, and while thicker armor is always good, you can make do with thinner armor as long as you angle the plates properly." Ibu knocked on the rivets positioned across the armor. "Set those up properly to make sure any round or attack is diverted away from where it could cause the most damage. Angle the plates right, and while the plates are, what, two or three centimeters thick, the round will have to go through them lengthwise, turning three centimeters into ten. Or more. Not a perfect system, but it's saved your life more times than you thought, I'll guarantee that."

Chill knew that already, but it was interesting to hear it from someone who knew what she was talking about. Ibu was as close to a master of the craft as they could find outside a factory and at a great price, too. She justified it by maintaining her old custom armor business and getting a little extra cash on the side from that while still earning a steady income for her work on their suits.

"You'll have better luck if you use some microfiber cloth and a bit of oxy-bleach solution to clean the inside," Ibu suggested as the rest of the crew made their way into the loading bay. "When you climb out, wash the inside pads with the solution, hit it with disinfectant spray, and leave it open to dry overnight. Won't take you fifteen minutes."

There was no point in asking Ibu why she didn't do it. It was on each of them to clean their own damn armor or live with the mess. Chill had always worked with armor that breathed, so sweat had never been a problem.

"When we're just off the job, I don't have the energy to clean my suit," Chill pointed out.

"Best time to clean it is right after it's been used. Plus, it lets the whole thing dry out before you get back into it. You can also start using fabric softener on the pads. It'll make them a lot easier to walk around in over longer periods and keeps them from building up a static charge."

She should have talked to Ibu about this a while ago. She took mental notes, although she didn't trust herself to remember any of it by the time they got back from their trip into Scourge territory. Still, she had the information. It was on her to use it.

Chill was the first one into her suit, quickly followed by the other two. The usual checks were run, and they were on their way out as the loading bay doors started lowering.

It was no surprise to see the Hammers waiting for them outside, decked out in full battle gear and raring to go. Chill wondered if they'd gotten any sleep since she'd seen them, but it wasn't her place to ask.

They did seem taken aback by the sight of the mechs marching toward them. After the problems they'd faced before, Chill had decided to leave a couple of mechs on the ship for defense unless they anticipated running into heavy resistance.

This time, they were heading into an area that had already been cleared out and doing a thorough sweep. Then they'd move onto the smaller compartments in the area to make sure the Scourge hadn't left any of its creatures behind for them to find.

In that case, they only needed a couple of the mechs,

especially since the Hammers were providing support on the run.

"It's one thing to see those big bastards on the vids," Blitz whispered, running a gloved hand over the side of Kortez's suit. "Another thing to see them in action. Not the kind of thing you expect to be running you down, eh?"

"Unless you're used to fighting combat mechs," Chill replied. "Anyway, show and tell is over. Time to sync our comms up and get ready to move."

The Hammers had had a day to acclimate and lose their jitters. It was time for them to show what they had to offer. Chill had all the faith in the galaxy in them being able to hold their own, but faith was not evidence.

The Hammers gathered themselves and followed the mechs as they made their way to an opening that led to the Verts they'd cleared. It was a good trip to get the new people started. There was probably going to be some Scourge presence, but cut off from their nest of origin, they would be easier to handle. It would also give them an idea of how to navigate the Verts. Once one was familiar, the others would be easier since all were constructed on a similar pattern.

Besides, now that their comms were linked, she could share the map of the station they had been updating from the old schematics. It was a work in progress, continually being fixed and worked out. All the teams had the program on their HUDs, which allowed a simple VI program to adapt the maps as they continued their exploration efforts.

One thing she hadn't expected to deal with was the Over-Keeper checking in with them. He didn't appear to keep the same rest hours as the rest of the crews, so she needed to test those hours to find out when he wasn't keeping a careful eye on them.

She found out Kuzratha was up and waiting for them in the early morning hours too.

"Over-Keeper, nice to hear from you this early." Chill kept her tone light and cheery as she answered his comm. "How can I help you?"

"I noticed you're heading out into the field with the new merc arrivals. I was surprised to find you hadn't apprised me of that."

She narrowed her eyes. "I wasn't aware that I needed to run my operations past you. Will you require that in the future?"

"Of course not. However, since they are the first merc crew to arrive at the station, I thought it would be best for me to be apprised of their status, as well as the kind of work they would be doing while you are holding their hands and keeping them alive."

Chill checked to make sure that they weren't on a team-wide channel. She knew they weren't, but it was a good idea to verify that.

"I'm taking them out to get the lay of the land as well as an idea of the dangers posed by the Scourge. Since we would do that anyway, I thought it would be a good idea to have them along to observe and back us up in case it was needed. Are you appropriately apprised, or do you need more details?"

"No, that is sufficient. Thank you for the details, Captain Chill. We'll be in touch."

Maybe she could have done a better job of masking her annoyance, and she couldn't tell if he was making a joke by calling her Captain Chill. That seemed like the kind of humor he would attempt.

"Fantastic. We'll drop you a line when we get back. Have a nice day, Over-Keeper.

"I'll look forward to it."

"In the meantime, you might want to focus on finding us a better option than the countervirus you gave us to work out the kinks in the Scourge's software."

"Naturally. There has to be something that will speed the process up." He smiled, showing that unsettling line of teeth before ending the communication.

"Freaks me the fuck out," Chill muttered.

"Over-Keeper have anything to say?" Dorian asked over the comm as they approached the opening.

"Just micromanaging me to the point where I'm starting to wonder if we might be better off killing him and blaming it on the Scourge."

"Ah. A bit early for that, don't you think?"

"What can I say?" Chill shrugged, and her suit shrugged with her. "I'm an overachiever in the morning."

CHAPTER SIX

"How old is the station, anyway?"

It was one of the other Hammers. Chill was slowly picking up their names, although it would probably be a lot easier if she just sat down and asked them, as well as things like what their stories were. Where they came from and where they wanted to be. That seemed like the kind of conversation that would go better if fueled by copious amounts of alcohol.

Of course, drinking together required they find themselves in combat together first. That was one of the unspoken rules of mercenaries, and she didn't make the rules.

"Nobody's sure," Chill answered, tapping on one of the hallway walls. "I mean, the Jindahin started putting the pieces together about three hundred years ago, from what I've learned, but there are a lot of conflicting reports on that too. It took them twenty-five to years put the station together, and I imagine that it took them another hundred to work out the scientific kinks of tapping three orbiting dwarfs for the power to maintain a wormhole."

"Oh, is that what that thing in the middle is?" Blitz shook his head. "I should have guessed, but we were more occupied by the state of the nebula. I don't understand why, but it was unsettling to look at."

She remembered the unsettling feeling, but there was no need to comment on it. There was something about this whole place that made them uncomfortable when they looked at it from the outside. It seemed to affect all the species that made their way to the station, so it wasn't an exclusively human problem.

"The station is estimated to be between a hundred and fifty and two hundred years old. It was considered a danger to the Jindahin's enemies, so after a couple of attacks that faltered against the defenses, they tried different tactics. They launched two viral attacks, one on the station's software and another on their biological makeup. That was more than they could handle, so the station was abandoned until the deckies started showing up under the promise of some old pirate's treasure being left aboard."

"There's treasure?" Scorch asked. She took a step forward and lifted her hammers from the hooks on her belt, flicking them on and off.

"Nobody's found any, but if you did, you'd be set for life." Chill tilted her head. "I can't remember the whole story. Some Jindahin general went pirate with his fleet, then went scorched earth on a couple of planets and a few stations before the Jindahin military decided they'd had enough and put together a military coalition to defeat him. As the story goes, he was defeated but managed to escape with the bulk of his treasure, which he stashed on the station with the help of the few connections he still had before slipping through the wormhole. That was before the station was abandoned, so nobody was able to chase him through the wormhole or find the supposed treasure.

"Is that the whole history of this place?" another Hammer asked. "We could find stuff like that on the cast nets."

"Well, yeah." Chill nodded, then motioned for them to head into the next chamber. "That's where we found most of it, plus some word of mouth from the deckies, although none of them know anything about the hidden treasure.

"I'd imagine that if one of them did find something worth enough to be called a treasure, they would keep it on the down-low. Just load it on their ship and leave. It's possible that there was treasure here at one point, but it was already claimed, taken away, and spent by someone who didn't want to be hounded to the ends of the universe for what they had."

That thought had come to her on one of the longer marches she'd gone on. It wasn't like there was much for them to do except think. The relays weren't working, so she couldn't watch or listen to something from the net to pass the time, and it was best that her attention was focused on the sensors anyway.

The Scourge could strike at any time, for any reason, from just about any angle. The smaller bots were more than capable of scuttling around in the air ducts, the water pipes, and any other nook or cranny. Since they weren't organic, they would only trip the sensors if they were out in the open where their general shape could be seen.

Aside from that, they could only be spotted or detected when they were active and moving.

They were approaching what had once been a business sector for trade and commerce, although she assumed its direct path from the docks meant that was where the military complex of the station had been set up too. That was why it was one of the first areas they'd pushed into after their first big engagement with the Scourge.

There had been a small nest in the chamber, but it had been cleared out before they attacked. It hadn't been an easy task, even with the nest gone. It had taken a combined attack by the DEMC crew and the Janissaries to wipe out the defensive bots.

"Big fucking place," Blitz whispered. "You thinking you'll be able to move the new arrivals who don't fit into Coil Cove into here?"

"That was the idea." She looked at the Scourge tower where the nest had been. "We're working on it, and I think we're making good progress, but nobody wants to move away from the Cove's defenses until we've set up equivalent defenses around here. We will need more people to do that. It's a conundrum, and while we try to figure out how to move forward, the Scourge tries to take the area back."

"If the AI can throw thousands of bots into a battle without fearing for its own safety, why hasn't it attacked you yet?" Blitz was full of questions, and they all sounded rehearsed as if he had spent the night before writing them down and asking himself in the mirror.

"We're not sure." Chill pinged on the chamber to check

for creepy crawlies, then highlighted the door on the far side. The space was the size of a small town, so it was quite a walk. They couldn't rush through lest they find themselves in the jaws of a trap.

"My working theory is that it has a finite resource pool, so it only moves when it has the resources to populate a given area with enough bots to defend it. We're in a stalemate until it gets more resources or we get more people. That's where mercs like you come in, hopefully to tip the scales in our favor."

"Hopefully" was the operative word. Having more crews was a good idea in principle, but Chill knew the mindset of the mercs. They might pick fights, develop grudges, and distract everyone from the greater danger. If there were more people, the chances of something like that happening were higher.

She'd been talking a lot. Kortez and Ivan hadn't chimed in to add their knowledge, which was substantial. They might be tired too. It had been an early start.

The door didn't look like much, but it was one of the more important areas in the Vert. Each chamber had dedicated control rooms that would have required at least a dozen people in each, working in shifts to ensure no part of the Vert was left unattended.

An AI could take over the controls, but only after the control panels had been suitably upgraded. The paranoia about AIs back in the day had caused the original builders to harden their UIs against artificial intelligence software.

Chill didn't care about that. Updating everything to make it functional was their employer's task, and he should be doing that instead of keeping track of their every move.

He was the one who wanted to use the station to generate whatever profits the Jindahin thought they could get from the place.

"Control rooms are through there," Ivan commented, pulling up the map and highlighting the area. "All three are interconnected through this central chamber here. In the past twenty hours, we've been losing our sensors in the area, which generally means Scourge activity. However, given the amount of electromagnetic activity on the station, they could just have gone haywire, so investigations are in order."

That was one of the details they left out of the vids. Dorian made sure those had enough data to keep people interested, but they were focused on the violence for the most part.

"Stick together," Chill called. "Keep your mind on where cover is at all times so you can get to it easily and quickly in the event of an attack. Your HUDs will help you set up overlapping firing lines to make sure we don't get swarmed. Let's go!"

They sported more firepower than their new partners, although Chill thought the Hammers would be a lot more effective in melee range. Their hammers would wreck just about anything that crossed their path. She wanted to see how effective they were at longer ranges with their casters, though. A few of them were fitted with longer barrels, which would give them better range. It didn't mean they were any good with the weapons, however, even though they were of medium-high quality. They were better than the caster Chill'd had when she was fighting Bugz.

Not as good as her coilrifle, though.

They knew how to arrange themselves in a tactically sound formation, but it was good to have them ready for combat anyway. They looked competent. They were keeping close to the walls, following the natural cover patterns as they moved through the area.

Their awareness was rewarded a moment later. As they approached one of the control rooms, her sensors lit up.

"Got movement," Kortez alerted her a couple of seconds later, highlighting the point for the rest of the squad. "Got…oh, that's a lot of movement."

"Looks like we tripped their sensors." Chill narrowed her eyes. There were only a couple of reasons, in their experience, for the Scourge to set up sensors. She didn't want to say that aloud because she was hoping it wasn't true.

"Are…are we under attack?" Blitz looked at his team. There was trepidation in his voice. The Hammers had paused, likely realizing they weren't watching vids anymore.

She pushed forward with Kortez. They took point while the Hammers defended their flanks, holding the line with Ivan and the two empty mechs. They would advance to the control room, but it appeared as though the Scourge would try to stop them however they could.

Chill was the first to shoot. She didn't notice she'd pulled the trigger until she saw one of the creatures take the round in the head. The round punched through and hit a creature behind it. Not thinking was the best way for her to hit her targets. Her instincts and muscle memory integrated perfectly with the automated interface with the suit.

It was mostly the suit, though. She assumed so, anyway.

Testing it would require seeing how well she could shoot when it was just her with a caster in hand.

But it was working in the field, so she wouldn't question it. Chill set herself up against a slab of prefab for cover and propped the rifle on top of it to steady her shooting hand, then fired as quickly as she could pull the trigger until the rifle started overheating. She replaced it with the other one and kept firing.

The barrage wasn't slowing the swarm. The bots that came in behind the first wave ran their comrades over or tore them to pieces if they slowed down.

"Hammers! Forward!"

Chill didn't dare look away, but her sensors told her the Hammers had broken formation and rushed forward to strike at the Scourge.

DEMC generally sent in grenades to stop the bots in their tracks, using the sudden decrease in momentum to shred those at the front and push the rest back. The Scourge might have picked up on their tactics and started to adapt to them, but they couldn't use that strategy anyway because the other mercs were attacking the lines, their hammers crushing the bots.

Several of the Hammers had interesting contraptions attached to their shoulders that fired their casters as they used their melee weapons, so they kept inflicting damage as they charged.

"They are...enthusiastic," Kortez noted. He hefted his rifle, carefully adjusting his firing lines to make sure they didn't shoot their comrades in the back. "Got to give that to them."

She nodded her agreement, left the defensive position

she'd taken up, and carefully lofted a grenade up and over the other group into the crowd of bots to give the Hammers more space to work.

As it turned out, their hammers were a lot more effective than she'd thought they would be. They clearly had plenty of experience handling them. The weapons rose and fell, crushing the bots one by one and spreading the pieces across the floor. Not a lot to be salvaged aside from the raw materials, but maybe that was for the best. Chill moved forward with them, pressing the advantage that the Hammers were creating.

"Hammers!" Blitz shouted, pointing his weapon at a new wave of bots. "Forward!"

They took his orders without thinking and threw themselves forward with battle cries that sounded like Kortez's, although they each had their own take. It was fascinating to watch, but they had to think about more than just proving themselves on the field of battle. They couldn't push forward too fast, or they'd end up surrounded by a horde of bots aching to tear into them.

Chill motioned for Kortez and Ivan to keep up with her but let the Hammers take point. That was the best way to see what the mercs could do, and it ensured that the DEMC wouldn't be on its own if the battle went badly.

"Keep them from getting themselves killed," she shouted, then motioned for Ivan to take the mechs into an overwatch position to find out where the attack was coming from. "Kortez, you and I are going to hold their flanks to make sure they don't get circled."

"On it, boss." Ivan offered a mock salute that was

imitated by the empty mechs. Dorian was apparently keeping an eye on their progress.

"Blitz, you better keep your people in line!" Chill shouted as the Hammer captain moved forward even though the Scourge was starting to retreat. "I'm not going to charge into a murder fest with you and your people!"

"We've got this!" Blitz told her, cackling softly. "They can't stop us!"

"They sure as fuck can," Kortez growled. "Get your people back in line now."

They were effective, but they were too enthusiastic. They needed to tone it down, or they wouldn't last very long on the Serpent. If they wanted to be aggressive, they needed to pick their moments. With the Scourge retreating, Chill wanted them to hold off on jumping into a fight they didn't yet understand.

"Ivan, what do you see from up there?" Chill asked when she saw that he was in position. "I have a feeling it's a nest."

"I...yeah. How did you know?"

"We wouldn't be running into this kind of resistance if they were just starting to take the area back." Chill shook her head. She hated being right, but knowing how the Scourge worked told her what she'd see, as predictable as the AI was. "It was trying to set up an advance staging area. Looking to circle around us to attack Coil Cove. We need to clear this area *now*. Dorian, are you following us?"

"I'm here, Chill," Dorian answered.

"Send a warning to the deckies. Tell them they might be looking at an invasion at any minute. We're going to head it off, but they should be ready for it anyway. In the meantime—"

"Yeah, yeah, I put a couple of fobs in your pack last night. Figured you might need them."

"I would say you're a doll, but we established that you don't like being called that."

Dorian chuckled. "I don't even know what it means."

"It…it means you're just what I need you to be in this case." Chill had no idea if that was where the term had come from. "Never mind. We'll contact you shortly."

"Can't wait, doll."

Chill rolled her eyes as she returned her attention to where the Hammers were gathering.

"How are you feeling?" she asked, studying the group. "The opening salvo might have been fun for you five, but the fighting will be a lot tougher from this point forward."

"Can't wait," Scorch yelled, getting whoops from the rest of them as she flicked her hammers into the air and caught them smoothly.

"We don't know much about nests," Blitz told Chill on a private channel so as not to dampen his people's enthusiasm.

"They're where all the bots are produced. They feed the raw materials in, and the nest brings it all together and shits out bots to give us a serious pain in the ass. They're usually well-protected and have some, shall we say, interesting defensive mechanisms. The last time we ran into an active nest, all the bots in the Vert suddenly got the order to tear the whole place up. That put the Vert in danger of collapsing and killing everything inside and possibly breaching the station."

"We introduced a countervirus that would allow us to see into the mind of the Scourge, as it were," Dorian interjected over what was supposed to be a private line. "Problem was when that CV hit, they sent out a termination code to all the bots in range."

Blitz nodded, not questioning how Dorian had joined the conversation. "I think I see. Hey, Cypher! Get over here!"

Cypher. That was a name for Chill to remember. She put it down as belonging to the sturdy woman who had turned her hammer into a poleaxe. She was a little taller than Chill and had a lot more muscle, which worked out well for her.

"Remember what you worked up with that EMP program?" Blitz asked. "'Hush,' I think you called it."

Chill shook her head. "Scourge shields their bots against EMPs. We tried that early on, and we needed to hit them three or four times to get anything to start frying."

"It's not an EMP as such," Cypher explained like she was talking to a child. "It cuts in on any electronic communication and turns it into static. Anything that's being broadcast over a determined frequency.

Blitz nodded. "If we can set it to the frequency the Scourge is using, could we use it to give your countervirus the time it needs to work?"

Chill tilted her head. It sounded like it might work, but Dorian paid the most attention to what the Scourge was doing. That was his job as they headed into the field. He wouldn't risk his life, but if he was drawing equal pay, he had to put in equal time and work.

"I guess it couldn't hurt to give it a try," Dorian finally

answered, not wanting to commit. "I mean, if we end up dealing with the same issue we had the last time. Ivan, you have a better grasp of how the hardware works. How fast could we get something like that running in this chamber?"

"It's a concentrated blast," Cypher corrected him.

It didn't matter. If it could be adapted into a wave instead of a beam, they could interrupt the Scourge's signals.

Ivan was muttering. She could not hear him over the comm, but she could see his body language as he stood above her. He even waved his hands to make his point.

"I guess it could work," he finally stated over the comm once he was done with his conversation with himself. "We need to understand that nothing is going to work out perfectly with the Scourge. I can fiddle around with it. A little help from Dorian, and we'll be able to get it up and running, no problem."

Chill nodded. "That's the beginning of a plan, then. Might be a way to keep the fucking bots from executing their usual self-termination sequence. All right, Cypher, you head on up and work with Ivan. The rest of us will prep for an attack on the nest. With any luck, we'll be able to press in before it can arrange its defenses, and Hush will keep it from being able to organize properly."

Hoping for luck wasn't going to work out if they didn't have another plan in the wings. Chill would also ask Ivan to craft a charge she could set up without his help that would bring the nest down in case the Hush program didn't work out.

She wasn't looking forward to handling explosives, but she would do what needed to be done.

At least the charge wasn't Plan A.

"And here I was, thinking you were taking us on a scouting trip close to home so we could get an idea of what we were facing here." Blitz shook his head. "Instead, we're trying to stop an incursion into Coil Cove. How exciting."

"Honestly, we *were* taking you and your team on a scouting trip. We wanted you to get a good idea of the kind of combat you and the Hammers are most comfortable with." Chill shrugged. "It would have been better if we could have done it in a situation where there was a little more control. As you can see, the Scourge has a way of hitting flanks we didn't realize we'd left exposed. We're glad to have the additional support. It'll take a while before the rest of the crews can arrange support for us, and this will be a major conflict. If you hadn't been here, we would have had to sit on our hands and wait for the others to come while trying to set up our defenses in case the Scourge decided to press its advantage."

Chill was thinking aloud since they didn't have much time to act. If the nest was active, the Scourge might attack Coil Cove in a matter of minutes. They would have no way to tell before their sensors told them about a wave of bots swarming toward them.

Most of the time, when Kortez and Ivan thought she was brooding, she was making plans. Having more people around made her talk about it instead of pondering things on her own.

"I'm excited to be in on this," one of the Hammers said. He was a large fellow, the one with the maul Kortez had his eye on. "Never been one to ease into things. Jumping feet-first into battle is more my speed."

She smirked. "Your enthusiasm is noted." That put more pressure on her. They were all looking at the DEMC to lead the way and have all the good ideas. If she had to keep her eye out for whatever crazy shit their new additions got up to, it would make things much worse.

Still, it was good to have their support, especially if they would be as active and aggressive as they had been in the first engagement. Chill had been surprised to see it, and she couldn't imagine how shocked the Scourge had been to find a line of hammers meeting their charge.

Ah, there she went, brooding again.

CHAPTER SEVEN

"Everything ready?"

"All good here," Ivan confirmed. "Just remember; the explosives I gave you probably won't be set off by anything other than the blasting caps, but they are still flammable. If something happens and they catch fire, throw them away since fire might trigger the caps."

"Right. Wait, *probably* won't be set off?" Chill looked at the pack she was carrying. "How probably?"

"Ninety-nine-point-nine-nine percent chance it won't go off," Ivan answered. "Incredibly unlikely, but still a possibility."

"Well, fuck." Chill took a deep breath to calm down and patted the pack. The explosive material was stable but attaching blasting caps changed that, so she would have to insert them when she wanted them to blow up. She did not look forward to doing that, but he'd wired everything already. Once the caps were in, they would connect to her HUD so she could set a timer or detonate them remotely, although he advised against the latter option since the

Hush program could interfere with her connection to the caps.

She took another deep breath. The bomb wasn't Plan A, but it was good to be ready in case Hush didn't have its intended effect and there was another attack on the Vert.

The Scourge hadn't yet reacted to their presence. If the nest had been preparing to invade Coil Cove, it would now refocus on defense. They had to attack and soon, or they would end up in a major battle. They preferred to attack before the nest could get ready.

The Scourge was testing their defenses, though. Probing and checking for weaknesses with lighter attacks to determine what they were up to and what their plans were, and how to turn those plans around on them during the fight.

This was the paranoia she'd been dealing with, although what she thought might be true. She motioned for people to approach the center of the chamber, where the tower was being rebuilt as they watched. Most of the structure had been taken down when the Scourge retreated the first time.

Chill realized that the building surrounded the antenna, which was probably the center of the nest and the purpose for its location. It would be nice if they could find out what the purpose was.

"Looks like we have our opening," Ivan announced. He was up on one of the few remaining buildings in the chamber, setting an antenna up with help from Dorian and Cypher. It would broadcast their Hush attack, although it would still be the job of the ground personnel to plug the fob so Dorian could connect with the network.

"All right," she whispered as she highlighted the point they would attack. "Let's get moving. Ivan, do you have any idea how many of the little bastards we'll be dealing with?"

"Tough to say," Ivan answered. "Won't be able to tell until they react to your advance. I'll keep you updated."

That was as good as it was going to get. The sensors in the area had all been disabled, which had kept them from noticing that the nest was being rebuilt. In the future, they would need a more reliable way to keep track of the Scourge's movements through the station.

That would be on the techies who would hopefully pour in with the mercs. They had Cypher and her Hush invention now, and they would soon find out how effective it was.

"All right, we have movement," Ivan noted over the comm. "Doesn't look like as many bots as the other nest had. Keep moving forward. They're on a defensive intercept course in your direction."

There had been no changes in the grav or atmo systems, so the Scourge wasn't trying to wreck the Vert… yet. The Scourge could still send that directive, so if the bots started to attack buildings and the like, stopping them would be her new highest priority.

Besides, having a Vert damaged this close to their base would cause problems. It might even force them to relocate if they couldn't quickly repair the damage.

The Scourge's plan made itself known when they reached the open area around the nest building. Bots of all shapes and sizes were swarming the tower's walls.

"I don't think climbing the tower is an option this time," Chill announced, motioning for Kortez to take point with the Hammers. "Time for us to find a more efficient way to attack the network."

"Roger that."

He sounded excited. She assumed it was not about optimizing their strategy, though. Rather, attacking with the Hammers had him raring to go. He wanted to see how he compared to the other mercs in an organized attack. Chill wanted to see what he could do as well, although she would stay back to direct the attack.

When the bots on the ground closed, Chill could see that while there were fewer in total, most were larger. They also sported heavier armor than the mercs were used to seeing. There were almost none of the rat-like creatures that had previously made up most of the swarms.

More felids with stinger tails were present, which she took to mean that this nest had been set up for an offensive. Their tails curled forward, the tips glowing as they fired a volley of white-hot stingers at the mercs.

"Get down!" Kortez roared. He pushed a couple of the Hammers out of the way just in time, although they might survive the stingers.

Chill's armor was largely unaffected, although if there were many attacks like that, the stingers would hit something vital. There was no point in giving them a chance. Chill opened fire on the bots and jumped into the fight ahead of the Hammers.

The mech suit really was good at that. That was not what it was designed for, but if they put in more armor on the front and installed a more powerful hydraulics system, each suit could be used as a tank.

There would be issues with doing that, but considering

that she was stomping through the felid bots with minimal damage to show for it, she'd explore the idea after this encounter.

She continued picking off targets with her rifle. She also drew her knife and slashed the heads of a pair of larger, bulkier bots. They'd been fitted with powerful hinged jaws, short yet stocky hind legs, and longer but less powerful-looking forelimbs. There was no tail on their slim and agile bodies. The creatures, about as tall as her chest in the suit, had been designed to be difficult to hit.

Their teeth glowed red as they lunged at her, looking to rip chunks of her armor off with those powerful jaws.

"Like hell." She jammed her knife in through the mouth and pushed, and the blade punched through the bot's skull. "That's a new one!"

There was no answer from the rest of the mercs. Chill realized she was deep within the ranks of the bots. They hadn't yet attacked, but they would. She yanked her weapon out of the bot's mouth and took the head off another bot that was trying to rip off the armor plate over her thigh.

Battle cries came from behind her as Kortez and the Hammers rushed over to join her. Her crewmate had been quick to realize her trouble. Cortador carved through the first of the felids that had survived Chill's assault, and the other mercs used their hammers on the bots they encountered.

There was no doubting their enthusiasm or dedication. She had distracted the bots, so the other mercs could jump in without taking much damage. Slugs pierced and hammers crushed bot skulls, forcing the Scourge creatures back step by step as Chill retreated from the swarm.

Kortez was having the time of his life. As Chill watched, he impaled a pair of the new creatures and lifted them off the ground. Then the Hammer with the maul cruised in and crushed their bodies with upward swings. He and Kortez worked together to great effect.

Scorch stepped in as well, and her hammers carved through bots as she gracefully and efficiently forced them back. Blitz also brought a dance-like element to his fighting style. Since he was older, Chill assumed he had trained Scorch. He only carried one of the hammers, pairing it with a caster.

She hadn't seen those moves before. No, she had—in the high-budget vids with the flashy fights where people fought in the air, kicking, punching, and sometimes bringing techno-magical powers into play. He stayed on the ground, though. Not much energy was spent on flips and fancy kicks, but his blows were elegant.

Chill was more than comfortable with her fighting style, honed as it had been for years in close-quarters combat, but she could always improve. She might ask him to demonstrate later. She gripped her knife tighter and joined the group around Kortez.

Some of the larger creatures were coming off the tower. There was no point in hating one bot type more than the others, but those were up there. They were larger than the suits they were wearing—not big enough to pose a physical threat, but the tusks or tentacles that jutted from the heads were dangerous. Dorian called them peelers since they could peel the armor off anything and anyone they ran into.

Chill pinged the information to Kortez. Though the Hammers were doing well at close-quarters combat, she didn't want to pit them against the peelers. The DEMC would clear the monsters off the field.

The big man nodded, pulled a handful of grenades out of his pouch, and tossed them into the bots' formation. That cleared a space between them and where the peelers were descending.

Chill used grenades as well, although hers would detonate on command instead of on a timer. Chill took a step back, sheathed her knife, and watched the peelers advance. They were slower than the felids and moved more ponderously, so their paths were easier to predict, even if their tentacles and tusks were harder to deal with.

Kortez cut one of them off, but that brought him a lot closer than Chill was comfortable having her people to those things. She ordered him back, then waited until the peelers were right on top of the grenades and Kortez was out of the way before setting them off.

She didn't expect the grenades to tear them to pieces. Damage was all she needed. Then she could snipe at them from a distance, and her slugs would penetrate.

More realistically, Ivan's shots would disable them. If their hydraulics leaked, those tentacles and tusks didn't work as well. That made it much easier for those on the ground to take them apart.

Ivan was doing a lot better than that; his shots were damn good. The grenades had made holes in the hard armor, and one of them was missing its head. Ivan cleared it from the field and did further damage to the ones that remained.

Kortez and the others dismantled the damaged peelers with their knives and hammers. They didn't destroy them since those bots had the most sophisticated hardware for salvage, and Kuzratha paid the most for their processors and circuit boards. Chill had no idea why he was so interested in their inner workings. She thought he might be sending them to Jindahin labs to study, not only to determine how to wreck them better but also to see if they could use their design in their own weaponry.

She doubted they would find anything groundbreaking. The peelers were similar to many living creatures, which was where the bots' designers got their ideas.

"All right, Chill, just like I told you," Ivan announced over the comm.

"Just like you told me," she whispered. She moved next to the tower, opened her suit, and climbed halfway out of it.

The air reeked of ozone and the fluid the bots used in their hydraulic system. It wasn't water, but that was all she knew. It stank, though, which made her think it had sat around for a while and was going rancid.

Ivan could probably have put the blasting caps in using his suit, but she couldn't risk it. Even if she was more vulnerable out of the suit than inside, it was better than blowing them all up if she dropped one of the caps. She pulled the charge out of her pack and carefully attached it to the tower's wall, making sure the adhesive was stuck to the surface before she massaged the malleable explosive. Ivan had told her that would make it more effective.

"That's it," Ivan commented over the comm. "Now all you need to do is put the two caps in. They're electric, and when they complete the circuit—"

"I don't need the fucking science, Ivan," Chill whispered. He couldn't hear her since she was outside the suit, but it felt good to say that out loud. She stuck the blue blasting cap into the blue explosives and the red cap into the red materiel. It was obvious, yes, but it had to be simple to arm the charge under fire.

Chill would bet some people got it wrong, and the explosives blew up in their faces because they weren't paying attention.

"*All right, the explosives are live,*" Chill shouted as she stepped back into the suit. Kortez and the Hammers were still keeping the area clear of bots. "Get back...how far was it again?"

"Ten meters minimum," Ivan told her and the other mercs. "And find cover. The blast wave might cause you trouble if you're out in the open."

She remembered that from the last one Ivan had set off. They headed for the nearby buildings as she keyed into the caps' frequency and set a ten-second timer after everyone was out of the blast zone.

The ground shook, and Chill felt the blast even from behind cover. The air was suddenly full of dust, making it difficult to see.

"Seems weird that we're now attacking nests every day," Kortez muttered on the comm. "Feels like the Scourge should be running out of resources by this point."

"It's only been two days," Chill answered as she stepped clear of the building she'd taken cover behind.

"When it happens for seven days in a row, I'll call bullshit."

"You attacked a nest like this yesterday too?" one of the Hammers asked.

"Much bigger than this one." Chill didn't want to think about having a gigantic creature waiting for them inside the tower. They would now have to anticipate that sort of thing when they attacked an active nest. Chill pinged the area but only picked on a handful of scattered bots, rats and felids from their size.

"Move in!" Chill called as she approached the hole she'd blown in the building.

Nothing was moving inside. That was odd in and of itself. She guessed it was because the nest hadn't been completed, so it didn't have the resources to spawn defensive bots. She saw chunks of creatures that had been close to the wall when the explosion went off. If they had been waiting to surprise anyone coming through the wall, it hadn't worked out well for them.

Chill advanced through the base of the building and located the node. She had the fob in hand, and when she was sure nothing was waiting to attack them, she approached it.

Kortez directed the crew into defensive positions around her as she slotted the fob into the appropriate port.

"Ivan, Dorian, you there?" she asked after it was in. "Fob is in. Let me know if you're getting this."

"I don't understand what we're receiving," Ivan admitted. "I guess that means you found the right one. Dorian, what are we looking at?"

Dorian didn't answer. Chill hoped it was because he

was analyzing the data and not because he was busy doing something else.

"It's incomplete," Dorian finally stated. "Looks like the Scourge is trying to take the nest down already. I can't tell if we interrupted them or if the AI decided this offensive was a lost cause and ordered their retreat. Either way, I'm mining it for all we can get. It's not going to take long."

"Roger that." Chill sighed. That was probably for the best. They didn't want to head into a major offensive without a lot more backup on hand, but she'd hoped they would be able to catch the Scourge with its proverbial trousers down.

She placed the explosives. If they were just going to bring the building down, they would do it quickly.

As important as salvage was, leaving the nest operational was a risk. For one thing, it would let the Scourge reclaim the area more easily. Even riskier was that they didn't know if the Hush program was working. The bots weren't tearing up buildings, but Chill couldn't tell if it was because the program was working or if they were abandoning the area.

"All right, I've gotten everything I can from the node," Dorian announced. "Blow that bitch and clear the area."

"Working on it." Chill set the timer on the explosives for five minutes, which would give them more than enough time to get clear of the chamber.

They moved quickly and quietly. Salvage would have to wait until they got rid of the tower. When they reached the edge of the chamber, they turned back to watch. The deckies who were rushing in to join the fighting came to a halt when they saw there wasn't any fighting waiting for them. They paused to watch the show as well.

There was a pregnant silence, then a loud crack and a flash of white light, which kicked the dust up again.

"Are...is that it?" Blitz asked.

"Wait for it," Kortez advised as Ivan and Cypher joined them. "Just wait for it."

Louder cracks echoed through the chamber as the tower sagged. It eventually dropped to the floor in a cloud of smoke and dust.

"I'll never get tired of seeing that." Chill grinned. "Dorian, any structural problems with the Vert?"

"Nothing yet," he answered.

"So, the Hush worked!" Cypher raised her hands triumphantly.

Chill opened her mouth to offer an alternative opinion, but she snapped it shut again. For all she knew, it *had* worked and there was reason to celebrate, so casting a pall on their win wasn't a good idea.

The group in the chamber cheered, including the deckies. Chill noted that Kortez carefully bumped chests with the Mauler.

"All good with you, Dorian?" she asked, connecting Cypher and Ivan to the conversation as well.

"Sure. The nest activated a few seconds after you connected the fob and flashed all its drives. I managed to intercept it with the countervirus, but most of what I got were fragments. I've been piecing them together. Have a look."

The data came up on her HUD, and Chill tilted her head.

"That's the Serpent," she commented. "Bits and pieces missing, but it's the Serpent's layout. I've stared at the schematics enough to recognize it. What are these markers?"

"I think they indicate nests," Dorian commented.

" I think that is unlikely," Ivan interjected. "That doesn't seem like the kind of data the Scourge would store in a nest that's under attack."

"It...it looks like a treasure map," Chill whispered, zooming in on one of the markers. "Most of their nests are in the larger chambers where the towers can be built tall, but these markers are in the control rooms. This is something else."

"A treasure map?" Ivan shook his head. "You don't mean—"

"We're not going to make any assumptions at this point," Chill growled.

CHAPTER EIGHT

"Lugosh. That was the asshole's name." Kortez was marching with the Hammers.

Chill glanced at him. "What?"

"Lugosh. That was the name of the pirate who supposedly left his treasure on the station." He nodded at the Hammers. "We were going to explore that when we got to the station to see out if there really was treasure left behind. Then, well, we ran into the Scourge, and that put all our plans on hold. Still, I think we should go treasure hunting. What do you think, Captain?"

She narrowed her eyes. He couldn't see her expression through her faceplate, but she was sure he could read her body language. The suit tensed when she did.

"Got something you want to talk to me about, Kortez?" she asked, raising an eyebrow. Lots of decky crews were gathering salvage to take back to Coil Cove. Considering how close it was to their home base, she was surprised more hadn't shown up.

"Just thought we might want to address your decision

that we weren't going to discuss the possibility of having uncovered a treasure map. If there was ever a time to talk about a possible treasure to be found, it's now."

Even if she disagreed, she would be outvoted. They were a democratic troop, and if they wanted to talk about finding Lugosh's treasure, they would, whether she liked it or not.

Besides, she owed Kortez one. She would have been trying to remember the pirate's name all day if he hadn't interceded.

"All right." She sighed and nodded. "We found a map of the station that might indicate where Lugosh's legendary treasure might be. Discuss away."

Ivan shrugged. "It's less fun if you just give in. We were expecting more pushback."

"I knew I was going to be outvoted, and I'm a firm believer in picking my battles," she answered with a small smile. "My question is why the Scourge would be interested in that. It's an AI, so it isn't looking to buy up land on a vacation planet."

Kortez and Ivan paused. Assuming they were thinking about how they would spend the treasure, Chill took that to mean she'd made a good point that warranted further analysis.

"Could be it just picked up something from a treasure-hunting crew that stopped by here many years ago," Kortez suggested.

Ivan was quick to disagree. "That wouldn't explain why we found it on the drives of one of their active nests. I'm no expert when it comes to the Scourge, but I'd say it's looking for whatever that map leads to."

"Come to think of it," Blitz interjected, "Kuzratha did mention that he would offer us primo pricing on locational data. Maps, schematics…anything recovered by the salvaging teams that would give us a better idea of the internal workings of the station. His words, although I suppose he might have something else in mind."

Chill pulled her helmet off and tucked it under her arm. "You think our Wayfarer is looking for Lugosh's treasure?"

"He never said so, but we could read between the lines. Kuzratha is looking for something very valuable that might have been hidden between the Verts."

She tilted her head. A Dahin Wayfarer looking for treasure on the station would not seem odd to the Hammers, but she knew better. He was Jindahin gentry, so treasure wouldn't be of interest to him, at least not for its monetary value. No matter how substantial the treasure was—and Chill wouldn't admit it was real—it wouldn't be enough to justify putting this much time and effort into the station.

Chill had known Kuzratha had his own angle, but it had never occurred to her that all he wanted was money. Unless there was something else about the treasure. Old tech that would help the Jindahin in their war, or possibly Lugosh had stolen or was in possession of a powerful weapon or tool that would give them an advantage.

Any of those would explain why he wanted the treasure, as well as why he had chosen to keep his desires from them. He would be getting them killed, and it would be an acceptable loss to him so long as he got what he needed. A few mercs killed by an ancient AI wouldn't matter much to him if the result was the Jindahin gaining the upper hand in the war.

"She's doing it again."

Chill offered Kortez her right middle finger. "Just thinking. That's not illegal, right?"

He grinned. "Come on. We were thinking about what the treasure might be. No reason for you to go wherever it is you go when your brow gets all furrowed like that."

"What's your theory?" she asked, raising an eyebrow.

"Blitz thinks it's mounds of precious minerals," Ivan offered. "Those would be worth more than creds to a pirate in a bartering system. If it's fuel, it would have decayed. Still, if there's enough material to build three or four cruisers from scratch, it would adjust their viability in the field of battle. I'm inclined to agree with him."

Kortez scoffed and shook his head. "No, no. If he had those kinds of materials on his ship, he could go anywhere in the colonized galaxy and use it to leverage himself into a city-state where he could hide out. If Lugosh left a treasure behind, it would be minerals and metals that were valuable but hard to move for whatever reason. My guess is that he got his hands on a massive supply of radioactive material."

"Wouldn't there be a radiation spike on the station?" Chill offered. Even if she had her doubts, the idea of finding treasure on the station was intriguing.

"Not if it was shielded," he answered. "There are a couple of ways to manufacture the stuff, and then it needs to sit for decades. If that was what Lugosh was transporting, it wouldn't have been viable for use then, but now that it's been sitting around, whoever finds it can use it. Just about everything we work with runs on a fusion reactor. A couple of tons could be transported on a ship and be worth billions of creds to the right buyer. What do you think, Chill?"

She didn't have a working theory anymore, not since she'd realized Kuzratha was trying to double-cross them. However, a new theory wasn't hard to come up with.

"Gold," she answered smoothly, seeing their confused expressions. "It's a heavy metal, so it's relatively rare in the universe, and a couple of the planets Lugosh attacked made their livings from extensive gold mines. It's a dependable conductor, a connector, and a heat sink on top of it. Most of the higher-quality ships use gold in their drive cores and their plating. It's a versatile metal that still has value in the jewelry community as well, so a few tons would be worth trillions, but nobody would want to buy it in that amount, especially if it's hot. Yeah, I'm going with gold."

It was a good theory. Even better because most of the treasure-hunting stories involved gold. Humans had an odd fascination with the stuff, which had made it valuable as a currency in history. In her modern interpretation, gold still had a very important place. In her opinion, anyway.

Chill shrugged. "Truth is, we don't know what we'll run into. I don't like the idea that we're going to have a bunch of mercs-turned-treasure hunters rushing into the jaws of the Scourge. People are going to get themselves killed, and I'll feel responsible. I'm entitled to a little brooding."

Kuzratha was trying to sneak them into a dangerous area of the galaxy with an agenda he hadn't shared with them. She didn't like that, but she expected it from him.

"What do you think we should do now?" Blitz asked, patting his hammer.

"I think we should keep the locational data we found

away from the Wayfarer for the time being," Chill suggested. "With more merc corps joining us, we don't need it becoming a free for all. People will start killing each other if they think they have a lead on treasure and they aren't in the mood to share."

Nobody disagreed, although she was surprised to find Blitz agreeing with her. He was looking to provide for his crew, and the creds from handing the map over would set them up with food and drink for at least a month.

"Word's going to get back to the bastard sooner or later," Kortez commented, studying their surroundings. "How long before we share it with him? Assuming we have the opportunity."

"When we know more about it," Chill stated after a moment of thought. "First, we don't know this is a treasure map, but if other people think it is, we'll have a stampede on our hands. We now have the means to approach the next nest without the whole fucking Scourge trying to wreck the station. We can push into another nest, tap the node, and hopefully dig up more information on the topic."

"My people aren't going to like that," Blitz noted. "They're going to want a payday for our work today."

Maybe he wasn't as supportive as she'd thought. "There will be plenty of creds from the salvage collected here today. I think I could talk Kuzratha into offering you a signing bonus too, since this was one hell of a trial by fire."

"Don't worry. I'll talk them down. That wasn't what I meant." Blitz shook his head. "What I meant was, my people know about the map, and they might take it to the Wayfarer. I just thought you should be aware of that. For the moment, though, we trust your judgment. You say the info stays with you, and we'll keep it quiet. We trust you."

He was speaking for his people, and Chill decided to trust him. She didn't trust the rest of the Hammers, though. Cypher knew about the map, so the rest of them knew too. If any of them decided they wanted extra pay for their work, they would sell that information.

Chill had a realistic view of mercenaries. Like Kortez had said, it was only a matter of time before someone handed the map to Kuzratha, which meant they had to find another nest sooner rather than later.

It would also keep the Hammers occupied and well-paid for their time, so it served a dual purpose.

Chill took a deep breath, straightened her back, and looked around the chamber. It felt like there was a piece of it missing from it with the nest gone, but she wasn't sure why. The nest had been a new building, after all. Still, with the scrubbers kicking in, the whole place was as clean as it was ever going to be. Teams were pulling chunks out and arranging for them to be transported back to the station by the empty mechs, which had been brought out to help.

Other transports were coming in to help as well, but they had to pick their way through the rubble. The suits moved more easily, picking up chunks and bits without getting tangled up like the rest of the transports would.

She shook her head, put her helmet back on, and picked up on the communications between Ivan and Dorian. They were discussing the other pieces of data they'd picked up. Nothing that needed her input, although Chill wanted to study the code the AI was using. It was reminiscent of code from decades ago, but it had evolved more than any of them had thought it would.

"I'm heading back to the Cove." Chill looked around. "Kuzratha is waiting for an update, and if we keep him out of the loop, it'll make things worse. Don't want him to think we're doing anything other than our regular butting of heads with him."

"Sounds about right." Kortez nodded. "Let us know how it goes."

"You act like I'm making enough money to justify giving me the shit duties." Chill shrugged. "That's fine. Just be aware that I'll remember, and I'll be delegating the shit duties to you."

"Oh, come on. Wait, me specifically or the whole crew?"

"The whole crew." She smiled. "You, Ivan, Dorian… Even Ibu. I've got my eye on all of you."

She was mostly joking. That wasn't to say she wasn't going to hold them to their word, though. If they kept sticking her with the task of keeping Kuzratha off their backs, she would get back at them.

But there would be no point in going too far with it.

She headed back to Coil Cove, moving against traffic since most of the people she encountered were going toward the new salvage field. There was still a lot of work to be done in the area.

It did beg the question of transportation when the station was fully operational. They mostly used the service hallways. Those were the lifeblood of a station, but they were generally filled with transports driven by VIs and AIs.

Up top, there were dozens of tunnels where trams and the like could transport the general populace, although it would take work to get those up and running again. It was a project for when the station had been taken back, although a professional would have to be brought in to deal with it. Given the age and the state of disrepair, much of the station would have to be replaced before more people could move in and work there.

Chill doubted she would be around long enough to see that. Not because they would be dead—although that was a possibility—but because their job would be done, and they would be elsewhere.

"Chill!" Shoviil waved at her. He was driving a PV that had been hitched to a string of carts. It was moving slowly, but it could carry a lot more weight than the PV on its own. "Good to see you were leading this attack. I hate to think of the Scourge being able to just pop up at random this close to Coil Cove."

"I know the feeling." She smiled as he brought the PV to a halt next to her. "Luckily, we were on it before the Scourge could set itself up for a bigger attack. I'm pretty sure any of the crews could have taken the tower down in the state it was in."

"I think you're giving us too much credit." Shoviil settled back into his seat with a grin. "There's plenty of salvage, though, and close to home, too. That's the bright side. You think we'll be able to stop things like this from happening again?"

"Stopping them might be too ambitious." Chill sighed. "We'll have to put sensors on all the approaches, radiating outward. The Scourge picks up on and takes out the sensors, but that in and of itself is a warning system. We'll need to be ready to counterattack every time one of the sensors goes down. We'll end up rushing out to find only malfunctioning sensors, sure, but we won't be caught by surprise like this again."

It did open them up to counterattacks. If the Scourge picked up on their reactions to a perceived attack, it might fake an attack from one side and surge from another. They would have to keep their specialized strike teams separate. DEMC would be one, the Janissaries another, and the rest would be split up between the new mercs as they came in.

The truth was, she was making it all up as she went along. Chill didn't know how to take a station, even if she was slowly succeeding. Her actions were based on her experience dealing with the Bugz as well as her panicked research into what had been done in the past.

"Well, we've got your back." Shoviil patted her shoulder. "Plenty of work to be done, but so far, it looks like you and your people are the ones for the job."

"I appreciate your vote of confidence, Shoviil." She smiled. "Go on. You're holding the line up."

She was right. There was a line halfway back to Coil Cove, and some of those waiting were getting impatient and peeking out of their vehicles' windows. They didn't shout or make noise to get him moving when they saw who he was talking to, though.

Chill wondered why. She didn't have a violent reputation compared to the rest of the mercs and the deckies.

Still, she waved Shoviil forward, and the rest of the line followed him. They *were* running a business, after all. They were organized enough to keep a solid line going to and from Coil Cove, with everyone driving on the left side. That left an avenue open for those who had to walk without disrupting the workers going out to the battlefield.

Coil Cove felt more like home than the merc stations on Mugh-9 ever had, although she'd never been one to put roots down. Maybe that was why she hadn't picked a name for her ship yet. She knew the 'Vette wasn't going to last long in their hands. They would find another mode of transport before too long.

"Captain Chill."

She turned to see the Over-Keeper waiting for her near his tent. He smiled and waved for her to approach.

"Kuzratha," she answered, pulling her helmet off again. "It's not—"

"I know, you're not the captain. I'm still not sure how it works for the five of you, but it does."

Chill smirked and opened her armor. It was the kind of conversation best held on even footing.

"I'm not sure how it works myself," she admitted. "They look to me for answers and decisions, but in the end, we make those decisions between the five of us. I defer to them if they outvote me. I'm not even sure how they decided I was the leader."

"Your soul," Kuzratha answered with a small smile. "It's a concept in my culture. The mind and the heart are constantly at war with each other over what the individual does. The heart is what the individual wants, and the mind is what they need. Neither agrees on much, so they turn to the soul of the individual to make a decision. Once the decision is made, time proves whether it is right or wrong and influences what the soul chooses next. Heart and mind blame the soul for bad decisions but take credit for the good ones. They still defer to the soul to make the decisions, though."

She tilted her head, and after a few seconds, she chuckled. "As philosophy goes, it's simplistic."

"True, yet it's accurate in the case of your crew. They turn to you to make the decisions and accept you as their leader because it is the easier route. It's not the privilege you thought it would be, is it?"

"Don't know. Don't care. We'll probably all be dead in a few months anyway, so it doesn't matter either." She crossed her arms and looked at the groups who were heading out to gather salvage. "Nobody wants it to be easy for the Scourge to attack. I guess it's best for them to focus on the bright side of easy salvage being close by."

"Indeed." Kuzratha gave that smile again, making it difficult to focus on anything but his needle-like teeth. It wasn't a natural gesture for a Dahin, but he'd picked it up to appear more natural when dealing with humans. "May we discuss how the Hammers performed in their first operation against the Scourge? Encountering an active nest must have been a surprise, albeit a welcome one."

"Not welcome, but it turned out in our favor. We caught the Scourge before it could set itself up to attack. I feel like I'm not considering it from the right perspective, though." She smiled as he offered her a warm drink. He had been enjoying one. "The Hammers were quite effective in the field. They handled facing the Scourge a lot better than I did the first time."

"Good. I'm glad they worked out. I think they would benefit from a bonus for their first job. A job well done, even when it proved to be more dangerous than they believed it would be. What do you think?"

Chill nodded. "That seems like a good idea. You can deduct it from my earnings on the job if you need to balance the books."

"That will not be necessary. You all earned what you're making for this job. The bonus will ensure that they know we appreciate having them with us." Kuzratha stared out at deckies who were heading out. "I put Shoviil in charge of supervising the harvest of defunct bots. He's been told to keep an eye out for intact processors."

"I doubt you'll find any."

"Yes, yes. The self-termination protocols fry every processor, but we will look for any that fail to do so."

She rubbed her temples. "You might want to consider a gesture of good faith for the new arrivals. It might be a good idea to pay us individually instead of by crew."

"That'll mean they get paid more than you do." Kuzratha narrowed his eyes. "A good-faith gesture?"

"It's fair. They risked their whole team to fight an unknown enemy. Rewarding them for that will encourage them to keep up the good work, like you said."

He nodded. "That is a good idea."

Kuzratha was suspicious. Then again, he was likely suspicious of everything and anyone he crossed paths with. Also, he was showing unsettling duplicity in his dealings with them, making their interactions difficult to judge.

They were interrupted by an alert from the dock that a new ship was coming in.

"More mercenaries have arrived," the Over-Keeper commented. "Most excellent."

"Judging by the state of their ship, they didn't pay much attention to the vids," Chill muttered, scratching her chin.

The ship was mostly intact, although it sported fresh scars from its battle with the Serpent's automated defenses. The DEMC had laid out the safe paths in their vids, and those warnings had been ignored.

"Shit," she whispered, turning back to her suit.

"Is something the matter?" Kuzratha asked, picking up on her urgency. "New mercenaries is good news, right?"

"Sure, but that ship's point defense systems are still engaged." She stepped into the mech again, drew her rifle, and started to move. "It means they're looking to start a fight. Even if they aren't, they'll get one."

She was proven right a few seconds later as the plasma cannons on the ship picked their targets. Deckies had been approaching the ship curiously, but they were quick to take cover once the plasma rounds started flying. Chill couldn't tell if anyone had been hit or injured, but it appeared as though the newly arrived crew was not expecting a warm welcome.

The cargo bay doors opened to reveal a group of heavily armed Xo-Trang who were ready for a fight. Their armor was heavy too, although not as heavy as the mech suit she was walking around in. They weren't looking to stop the fighting but rather pointing their weapons at individuals and shouting in their native tongue.

Shouting was an odd choice. They had come in hot, and now they were trying to talk to people? The ship couldn't take much more damage in the state it was in, and while they weren't trying to surrender, they did appear to be trying to open a dialogue with the locals.

Chill stepped out and opened fire on a cannon that had swiveled around and pointed at her. The tungsten round punched through the cannon's barrel and damaged its circuitry. It tried to fire anyway, but the superheated round melted through the holes in the barrel and caused more damage to the ship.

"Dorian," she shouted, ducking behind a stack of heavy crates as two more cannons swiveled to point at her, "Let Kortez and Ivan know we have trouble at the Cove."

"Done and done. They were on their way back, so they should be with you in a couple of minutes. In the meantime, Alex and I are trying to take their point defenses down before they cause any more damage."

"Fantastic." She checked her rifle and directed her attention to the Xo instead of their defense systems when she stepped out.

CHAPTER NINE

She wasn't going to be alone. Kortez and Ivan were coming to help, and the Janissaries were approaching from the other side.

As nice as it was that she wasn't alone in the fight, they would annihilate anything and anyone shooting inside the docking area. Chill didn't think that was a good idea if these mercs just needed time to adjust to the fact that not everything on the station was trying to kill them. If they still wanted to start a fight after they figured that out, she would be more than happy to oblige.

There was no point in assuming they wanted to fight, though.

Chill raised her hand to stop the rest of the crews from attacking and gestured for them to take cover as she stepped out. The ship's cannons tracked her as she approached.

"My name is Chill," she announced, letting the suit's external speakers give her voice emphasis as she approached the Xo. "I'm with the Dead Evil Mercenary

Company, and you're pissing me the fuck off. If you really want to start a fight, I'm more than happy to oblige. If you don't, lay your weapons down and disable the point defense systems on your ship. You have thirty seconds to comply, or we'll assume you have violence on your minds."

If these mercs had been drawn to the station by their messages, stating her name and the name of their company should calm them down. If they still attacked, they would pay the ultimate price for it.

The Xo crew backed away from her with terrified looks on their faces. It took her a few seconds to notice the empty mechs moving in behind her, weapons out and ready to attack. Chill assumed she had Alex to thank for the backup. The others were on the way, but being flanked by half a dozen heavy suits was impressive.

For a second, it didn't look like the Xo would cooperate. They were too well-armed to be a random merc crew looking for adventure, and if they picked a fight, it wouldn't be easy to drive them back into their ship.

Finally, one of them raised a hand and barked orders in Xo. Given their response, he had ordered them to lower their weapons but be ready to fight. Chill maintained her position in front of the loading bay doors. Putting on a show of force was one thing but making them think she was going to take over their ship was another.

The apparent leader came over. Her suit made her about a half-meter taller than him. She wasn't often taller than Xi- or Xo-Trang, since their long, slender bodies let them look down on almost every other species they encountered.

Physically and psychologically.

"Good choice," Chill commented and crossed her arms. "Now, is there a reason you came in guns blazing?"

The leader looked up at her, then pulled his helmet off, revealing the hardened scar tissue on the top of his head. The Xo-trang had their feather crests removed—often forcibly and always painfully—to cut them off from the Xi-Trang by eliminating the ability to psychically communicate with them.

Chill had never understood how they justified the mutilation, but it was far from the craziest thing she'd seen in the universe.

"My name is Hithaal," the Xo answered, placing his hands on his hips. "I represent the Harvest in this endeavor."

"Did he say the Harvest?" Dorian interjected over the comm.

"Yep." Chill recognized the name too. Trang crews preferred the definitive article and a strong noun, so most of their names sounded the same, but the Harvest had a reputation.

"As in, the assholes that even the extremists among the Xo think are too much?" Dorian continued.

"The very same." Chill shook her head. She was being rude to the Xo in front of her. The truth was, their reputation varied depending on who was talking about them. She had heard they were a horde of treacherous, atrocity-happy pirates who didn't care who was hurt so long as they got paid. She'd also heard they were honest and honorable hard cases.

Reputation, as they all knew, was just gossip. Chill learned long ago that while it was a good idea to learn about the people they were dealing with, it was best for them to form their own opinions.

Chill turned her attention back to Hithaal. "This is the part where you explain why you came in like you wanted to wreck everything in your path. She still wasn't clear on how to pronounce his name.

"We came to this place for the work on offer," the Xo answered, gesturing at his ship. "As we approached, we were targeted by the station. The cannons on the surface forced us to maneuver past the ships guarding the entrance before they could target us as well. Once that happened, we expected to have to hack our way through the rest of the defenses."

Chill made a mental note to check on the guardian ships to find out why they had allowed a ship to slip by them without raising the alarm. Still, she could now understand where the Xo was coming from. They had landed on the station with the same thoughts in their minds.

"You could have avoided the damage to your ship and wouldn't have had to fight if you had paid attention to the vids we put up," Chill noted, tilting her head. "We put a lot of effort into explaining how to approach the station and tap into the guide that would let you avoid the active defenses."

Hithaal raised an eyebrow at her. "Vids? What vids?"

"The vids we posted on our channel." She narrowed her eyes. "That *was* what brought you here, right?"

"No. Our company sent us here on an exploratory mission to assess if it would be worth the time and effort. Hence just the frigate and a half-crew."

"Oh, the Over-Keeper isn't going to like this," Dorian

whispered as Kortez and Ivan rushed over. "You think he's not happy now? Just imagine his mood after he finds out the Harvest is sniffing around his station."

"Doesn't matter what he thinks," Chill answered, keeping her conversation with Dorian private from the Xo. "Unless he makes an official declaration that identifies the station as belonging to the Jindahin, he doesn't have any say over who can or can't be on it."

That didn't simplify matters, though, and they didn't need another group making things even tenser with their employer. It didn't matter if it was a small crew. Kuzratha would send a message to the Harvest that their interference was not welcome now or ever.

That meant someone would try to kill the Xo. Killing the messenger sent its own message.

She wasn't happy about the situation either. The Harvest, as far as she knew, was a much larger operation than they were used to dealing with. They had all sorts of political ties to make things even more complicated. Since their dealings with the Red Crows and the Pit Lords, she was leery about associating with the larger organizations.

Also, Hithaal thought a small crew consisted of a dozen well-armed mercs, which told them nothing about the crew on the ship.

Even with the Hammers, the Harvest had the numbers to pose a significant danger to the rest of the crews, although the deckies would probably be effective at stopping them if they put their minds to it. Given the way they were watching the Harvest mercs, it would take a while before friendships blossomed between the sides.

That meant it would take a lot of work to get them

functioning together without fighting, and everyone would look to her to resolve their disputes.

Plus, she knew the decky crews could be fickle, so there was no telling if they could count on them when the time came.

"Right, well." Chill cleared her throat and pulled her helmet off as a first step toward keeping hostilities from breaking out. "Welcome to Coil Cove. If you stay here, you'll be expected to work like everyone else. If you don't like that, feel free to hop back on your ship once it's been repaired and head back to your superiors. We won't tolerate freeloaders around here, not when we have an enemy at the gates."

"What enemy?" Hithaal asked, raising an eyebrow.

"You really should have watched the vids," Kortez suggested. "All the details are there, and there's plenty of fun and gratuitous violence to keep it interesting. Also lots of epic one-liners, although those might not be as interesting for you."

"The short of it is, we are dealing with an ancient AI function that has been creating bots and trying to take over the entirety of the station," Chill explained. "He's right. The vids do a good job of showing you what you'll be facing in this fucking place. The point is, there's a lot of money available and a lot of danger to go with it.

"If you stick around, you'll subject yourselves to both. Watch the vids and decide if you want to stay. If you do, we'll expect you to pull your weight, and considering you come with what appears to be a well-armed and battle-hardened crew, that's going to be a lot of weight for you to pull."

"I understand." Hithaal nodded. "It looks like you run a tight ship."

"It's not my ship, and it's not my station. We're newcomers to the Serpent ourselves, but you quickly learn that if you don't get in step with the rest of the crews around here, you get killed, and you get other people killed."

That got a smirk from the Xo. "We are quick learners; of that, I can assure you."

Kortez tapped her shoulder gently, and she saw the Over-Keeper approaching. He was dressed in the rich robes that helped him pass as a Wayfarer, although she wasn't sure how well the disguise would work among his kin. The Dahin in the decky crews hadn't raised any questions, although Chill never could get a straight answer from them as to whether they were Wayfarers themselves or they were aligned to any of the denominations. They always said they didn't want to involve themselves in politics, which Chill assumed meant they were Wayfarers. However, none of them liked it when she put it that way.

She was better off not talking about it. They took their designations seriously and didn't appreciate outsiders trying to do it for them. It was a personal choice.

"Welcome, Harvesters," Kuzratha offered a deep and elaborate bow with his greeting. "New faces are always welcome on the Serpent, my friends. I am Kuzratha, a humble Wayfarer hoping to reclaim the station of his forebears. I promise, Captain Hithaal, that you and your crew will find a great deal of promise and profit on this station. My abode is open to all who have a mind to discuss business, and there is a great deal of it for those who come prepared to fight their way through this place."

He was speaking their language, it appeared. Talking about money took the hostility out of their eyes, and they relaxed. It was the universal language of mercs. There were other rules, of course, but in the end, creds talked while bullshit begged its way into the economy frigates.

"I look forward to discussing business opportunities with you." Hithaal bowed his head with a small smile and motioned for his men to holster their weapons.

Everyone calmed down. The deckies were still worried, but they were more concerned by the damage that had been done to Coil Cove when the Harvest ship arrived. Not all was sunshine and roses, but it didn't look like they needed to worry about an invasion.

Kuzratha was still speaking to the captain, and Hithaal invited him into the ship for a private conversation. She wasn't going to tell the Dahin what to do, although she knew better than to walk onto a strange merc's ship. That was doubly true when they had been pointing their weapons at everyone else minutes before.

If their employer ended up dead, they wouldn't get paid and would likely lose the support of the Janissaries. That was all Chill cared about, although she knew she *should* have cared about his wellbeing.

Kuzratha's seeming disregard for the DEMC's wellbeing made it easy for her to quell the empathetic instincts that rose in her.

The crowd dispersed, and Chill suddenly felt tired. It had been a long day, even if it was only halfway through the day phase of the station's cycle. She had noticed that she got tired more often the longer she was on the station. It was time for her to look into that.

The Janissaries watched their boss head into the strangers' ship. They didn't look like they were worried about his safety.

"I thought you would insist on going into the ship with him," Chill commented when Commander Kharkanaw pulled his helmet off. The Janissaries didn't do that unless they felt relaxed.

"We let him go into *your* ship when we met for the first time," the commander answered, raising an eyebrow.

"Sure, but we're decent people, no matter what you might have thought of us at the time." Chill grinned cheekily. "If he runs into trouble while he's in there, he'll be dead before you can reach him."

Kharkanaw shrugged. "If that's the worst they can do, I can live with that."

"Aren't you supposed to keep him alive and well?"

"Sure, but if he keeps pulling dumb shit, we won't be blamed for it. That's the quickest way to get us off this godsforsaken station."

The commander clearly wasn't happy about where their career choices had led them, which wasn't a surprise. They were trained to be on the front lines in any conflict their species engaged in, and instead, they were babysitting a dignitary. Clearing the station was dangerous, but it fell well short of the kind of glory they had been hoping for when they joined the Janissaries, or so she assumed.

If they weren't worried about the Over-Keeper's safety, she wouldn't be either. She motioned for Kortez and Ivan to head back to their ship, followed by their empty mechs.

"Yeah, yeah," Chill growled as they entered. "I'm brooding." She stepped out of her suit and collected the products Ibu had suggested she use to clean the suit after she was done with it for the day.

"You know, when you pre-empt our teasing, it takes some of the fun out of it," Ivan commented. "Not all of it, mind, but some."

She grinned and got to work cleaning her suit. "I'm sorry. Well, not really. Just tired, so I thought I'd cut to the meat of your jokes so you could get it all out. I'm brooding and deep in thought. Let's get it over with."

"I think your tiredness has a cause," Zichix chimed in before the other two could get a word in. "I've been keeping track of your health signatures, and you are all under a great deal of stress."

"This is going to be a segue into you talking about procedures again, isn't it?" Kortez predicted. He patted his kid on the shoulder, or rather, what he had instead of a shoulder—the joint that connected his upper limb to his thorax.

"Why, yes, it is. How intuitive of you, Dad!" He preened before turning his attention back to Chill. "I've been thinking about how to keep track of your health state. The suits are designed to do that. Their readouts are basic, but those are better than the invasive tests you would otherwise have to undergo. With a little help from Alex, I can collate the data."

"Interesting," Chill muttered. "You only came up with that idea after you got a negative response to the tests you suggested. If those are really necessary, you can order us to undergo them."

"Really?"

"You're our medical officer. When it comes to the health of the crew, your word is law. You know, within reason."

No point in letting the kid get too power-happy. If she gave him a blank slate, the rest of the crew would balk.

"You think we should have stuck around with the Over-Keeper while he was dealing with the new guys?" Kortez asked. "I don't think they're going to hurt him, but if they want to take the station over, it makes sense to start by taking hostages."

"He's not our problem," Chill reminded him. "If they try anything funny, they'll have the Janissaries to deal with. I don't need to remind you what they do to people who piss them off."

Kortez didn't look convinced, although she couldn't tell if it was because he was concerned for the security of their employer or disliked the Harvest.

"Nothing we can do about it now." She finished cleaning the inside of her suit and left it open to dry. "The Over-Keeper knows how to take care of himself, and he has his own security forces. But keep talking about it, and maybe your kid won't decide to probe us."

Ivan grinned and got a scowl from Kortez. Zichix seemed unaware of her annoyance as he connected to her suit and called up a handful of panels.

"If we're going to be talking about something else," Chill continued, stretching and rolling her shoulders, "we could talk about what we pulled off the nest's drives. Right, Dorian?"

"What?" The youth had come down from the cockpit to join them. "You want to keep talking about the map?"

"Unless there's anything new to discuss, no." She sighed. "The map isn't the only thing we got from the nest, right?"

"No, but we're still not sure what the fuck else we picked up," Dorian explained. "Considering that we're putting as much time and effort into keeping the Scourge software from infecting our system as we are into deciphering the data, the process is slow."

"Well, let me know when you have something." Chill rolled her shoulder again; something was pinched and uncomfortable in there. "In the meantime, I'm going to take a shower and get some food."

"You're going to leave all this work for us?" Kortez asked.

"Hey, them's the perks of being the captain." She offered him a mock bow. "Let me know if you need me for anything, but if you call me for something you could have handled, I will be cranky."

"Noted."

Maybe being captain had a good side. Sure, everyone thought she had all the answers, but she could just hand the busy work to someone else while she took time off.

It wasn't going to last, but while they tried to understand what her role as captain meant, she would be able to boss them around.

A hot shower and a steam, followed by a meal, would hit the spot. Chill doubted she would be back up to full capacity, but getting close was fine.

Maybe she could sleep in and take a day off while the rest of the crews retrieved the salvage from the nest. Hopefully, by that time, the repair crews would have already fixed the other chamber they'd cleared and they'd have more than enough work to keep the Hammers and the Harvest occupied and well-paid.

It probably wasn't the kind of work they'd thought they would be doing on the station, but it wouldn't be long before they were all wishing they were scavenging instead of dealing with the Scourge.

There wasn't much in the way of fresh food for her to work with, and Chill didn't feel up to reconstituting the flash-frozen food in their cargo bay. Leftovers were all she had on hand that could quickly be heated up for a snack.

Her hair was still dripping, but Chill wasn't going to put herself through the trouble arranging it. At least her silver locks were short and easy to manage.

"Come on, Dad! It's for your health!"

"Fuck off!"

Kortez, wearing nothing but a towel wrapped around his waist and dripping wet, ran down the hallway, followed by Zichix.

"Humans are annoyingly bad about conserving their health," Zichix pointed out. "I'll try not to make them too invasive, but tests are required. I'm not going to let you poison yourself."

"I was taking a fucking shower, not rubbing belladon oil all over myself."

Chill grinned and shook her head. Kortez continued moving down the hall away from Zichix.

"What's going on?" Ivan asked. He hadn't taken a shower yet, so he still reeked of stale sweat. Chill was a little too aware of the smell now that she was clean.

"I'm going to guess that Zichix tried to run some tests on Kortez while he was in the shower, and Kortez objected." Chill shook her head. "Now Zichix is reminding him that there's a lot more at stake than his personal comfort."

"What kind of tests, do you think?" Ivan collected some food from the cooler and didn't bother to warm it up before digging in.

She wasn't sure what he was eating, although it smelled like protein paste and grain. Chill wasn't going to manage what her crew ate. It would be hypocritical for her to complain about the Over-Keeper micromanaging their every move, then tell her people what they could and could not consume. However, if Zichix complained on the basis of the crew's health, she would have to make changes.

"It looked like a scanner," Chill pointed out. "It's what they use to take skin samples and test for anything from eczema to skin cancer. Kortez is just being a bitch about it."

"Fuck you two," Kortez snapped as he came in, holding onto his towel. "If it was just a skin sample, why the fuck were you getting the sample from—"

"You had an abnormal mole in the region that needed to be tested and tracked," Zichix explained as he followed Kortez into the room.

Dorian came in as well, mouth frozen open as he tried to figure out what was happening.

"Don't ask," Chill advised, taking a bite of her snack.

"I just... Why is Kortez—"

"I said, don't ask," she insisted, motioning for him to get closer. "What's up?"

He shook his head. "Just looking over the data we mined from the nest before it shut down. Most of it's jumbled and incomplete, and I've been trying to put it together. Chunks require access to their home server before being opened, so the next time you plug the fob into one of the nests, I might be able to unscramble more. Besides that, though, I think I've identified one of the locations on the map. Narrowed it down, anyway. The bits we collected aren't as incomplete as we thought. Just need some creative rearranging."

"He's going to start talking about how skilled he is again, isn't he?" Ivan whispered.

"Damn straight," Dorian shot back. "Anyway, here's the location I found. No idea why it's cited on the map. There's nothing to indicate what we'd find if we went there, but, well, it seems like the kind of thing we'd end up doing."

Chill raised an eyebrow. "We?"

"I'll be there with you. In spirit. Piloting the mechs."

"It'll be a nest," Ivan stated. "Heavily defended, and not the kind of spot the Scourge will be willing to give up. Might even be a central hub for the other nests radiating out from it."

"We're going to attack it anyway, aren't we?" Dorian muttered, crossing his arms. "We should start looking at ways to confront the Scourge on a larger scale. If we keep this slow fighting up, we'll all end up dead."

CHAPTER TEN

Dorian was right. If they kept fighting the Scourge slow and steady, eventually, the Scourge would figure them out and press a lot harder. It had the advantage of numbers.

Chill didn't want to commit them to a move that would get them killed, which meant the decision would have to be made by all. They could stay on the Suneater for the foreseeable future, but even with new mercs showing up daily, they might have to fight the Scourge for decades before they reclaimed the station. That assumed the AI didn't adapt to the new arrivals.

It also assumed they didn't die. That was a possibility mercs had to accept, and she didn't take it lightly.

"The Hammers are here," Dorian announced over the intercom. Chill was watching replays of their fight. She had to keep improving their form for future fights, but she was having a hard time focusing. She'd made notes for herself and Kortez, which would justify the time she'd spent watching the footage. She hadn't just been sitting around, wasting time.

"Bring them into the cargo bay," Chill answered, pushing off her bed. "We're going to need privacy." She had called the meeting, and now she would see if the newcomers would join them.

"Will do."

The Hammers had just arrived, but they had been here for long enough to be aware of the dangers waiting for them. Chill didn't want to make any assumptions about what they would involve themselves in, but the group was crazy enough to want in. They liked jumping into fights with hammers, which said it all.

They weren't any crazier than Chill and the DEMC crew, and considering she had suggested the mission, she had no right to call other people crazy.

They would find out what kind of nuts they were dealing with in a few minutes.

Blitz saw her come in. Kortez and Ivan were already there, commenting about how the fighting had gone. One of them was showing Kortez his hammer.

"Captain Chill," Blitz called, which got the attention of the others. "We were surprised to receive your message. My people and I were about to get some rest in before preparing for another go."

"I appreciate your willingness to speak to us," Chill answered. "And I'm not the captain."

"Right. Sorry."

She smiled and motioned for them to sit. "We've been digging… Well, Dorian's been digging through the data we collected from the nest. From what he's told me, it's a jumble even the Scourge has a hard time parsing, but he did manage to identify a location that is marked on the map.

"The Scourge thinks it is important. We're assuming there's a large nest in that area, a central node the other nests are stemming from."

Blitz nodded as she called up a holographic image of the area in question. "Lots of power nodes running through that sector. It would be a good spot to power their production lines from. But why are you telling us about this?"

"Considering we found this intelligence together, I thought it was only fair that we bring this plan to Kuzratha together." Chill shrugged. "There is a new element in the area, and we can't counter the Harvest on our own if they prove to be a threat. They're an unknown factor."

"You want to take this to Kuzratha together." Blitz looked like he wasn't sure what she was suggesting.

"We have to keep a lid on the situation, which means we need to take it to him together, yes. At least keep a lid on our plans to move on the location."

"I see. So, you'll be sharing the data you collected with Kuzratha?"

"We wouldn't be able to advance through the area without his support, especially if there's an arch-nest to deal with. It will be difficult, and we're going to need the Janissaries' support to get it done, even if we're going to keep a tight lid on the situation."

Blitz nodded. He wasn't stupid. He knew there was more to the situation with the Over-Keeper than they were being told, but he wouldn't push for more information just yet. They were the new kids, so pressing for more than they were offered would backfire on them.

Chill knew it wouldn't work out the way they wanted it to. If Blitz felt like he was being played, he wouldn't trust them either. She didn't like politics, and if she was going to put people in danger, she wanted them to be fully informed about the situation before they went into it.

"Let me know when you're going to have a conversation with Kuzratha. We'll be there to support you." Blitz nodded, took Chill's offered hand, and shook it firmly.

"I appreciate it, Captain Blitz." She smiled as he directed his people out of the bay. Shoviil was waiting outside for them to finish.

"Busy day for you, huh?" he began, waving at the departing mercs.

"Nice to see you again, my friend." Chill motioned for him to take a seat. "Is it good to see your people joining our party?"

Shoviil shrugged and ran his fingers over the scars where his crest had once been. "The Harvest isn't what I would call 'my people.' Never saw much of them, and what I heard didn't put me in a trusting mood. Besides, I left the Xo behind a long time ago."

"You never did say why you left them to come and join a bunch of pirates." Chill shrugged. "Not that you have to tell me anything you don't want to. Still, I can't imagine the situation was any good if you gave it up to deal with the Scourge and Lugosniffers like us."

"I thought we had established that you and your crew aren't Lugosniffers." Shoviil tilted his head. "Although the word is, that might change."

"Word might be right."

Shoviil smirked. "Well, it should interest you to know that the repair crews got the self-repair systems working again. Their efforts focused on repair rather than salvaging, but the creds you gave me to give to them more than covered the costs. If you're going to want more people to salvage the other nest you found, you might want to have a word with our good Wayfarer about spreading more creds around to make sure people don't complain about the division of labor."

"I will. He's busy at the moment, talking to the Harvest about what he wants from them."

Shoviil's eyes narrowed, and he glanced at the open door like he was thinking of making a quick escape. If he wanted to leave, that was his choice. She would respect it and him.

"Have you ever dealt with the Harvest?" Shoviil finally asked, raising an eyebrow.

"No," Chill answered honestly. "But I've heard a lot about them. Some of it good, some of it bad. Hard to tell what the truth is from how their rivals describe them."

"Sure." Shoviil nodded. "Still, they are known for being ruthless. Be careful dealing with them. They will look out for themselves and only themselves. They don't even care about the other Xo in the galaxy. They've been known to leave their own people high and dry without a second thought. They're infamous among the Xo-Trang, even though most of us see it as our duty to help others of our kind who have suffered under the control of the Authority."

Chill nodded slowly. "I appreciate the warning, Shoviil."

"Sure. You saved my life, so I should see to it that you're around for a while to keep on doing so."

She smirked. "I'll keep you alive long enough to return the favor."

"I appreciate it. Anyway, I should get back. You people always make a big mess when you deal with the Scourge, so there's plenty of salvage for the deckies."

"Have fun with that."

Chill watched Shoviil jog off the ship. From what she'd heard, he wasn't doing much salvage himself. The rest of the crews were paying him to coordinate their efforts. He had become a leader in his own right.

His efforts were appreciated. Most of the deckies trusted him to have their best interests at heart since he was one of them. Besides, he knew how they worked things out, so it was for the best.

"You really think that bringing the Over-Keeper up to speed will help?" Kortez asked. He settled into a seat next to hers and started to work on his suit.

Ibu did most of the maintenance work, as well as making sure that they had the spare parts to replace the plates and pieces that couldn't be repaired. Still, it was a good idea to work on their own suits too. They never knew when they would have to repair them in the field.

It was Chill's idea, although it had gotten enthusiastic approval from Ibu. Chill assumed that was because she wanted time off. It wasn't a requirement, though, so if they were otherwise engaged, the suits were still Ibu's responsibility.

"Chill?"

She remembered that he had been speaking to her. "Ah,

right. I mean, it's not much of a change from our current situation. Besides, we know the asshole will find out eventually, so we should share it with him on our terms. We still don't know what his future plans for us and the other teams on the station are, so I want to see his reaction when he learns what we discovered."

"Seems like playing with plasma to me." Kortez shook his head. "The asshole didn't hire us to look for treasure, which means any we find is ours. He shouldn't have anything to do with it."

Chill wanted to disagree with him, but Kuzratha had sent them in with less than the entirety of the intelligence he had available to him. She could understand him wanting to play things close to the vest—or that odd, ever-shifting jewel-encrusted robe he wore—but he couldn't expect them not to do the same.

Still, if she knew the Dahin, he would have a hissy fit about not being told everything. He was a hypocrite, but they knew that.

"Send word to the Hammers," Chill stated on the intercom, pushing up from her seat. Kortez closed his suit. "No point in delaying. Besides, if the Scourge somehow finds out what we know, we won't have the chance to attack the arch-nest or whatever the fuck it is we found."

"*I* found," Dorian countered with a tight smile.

"Right. You got it off the fob I put in while fighting for my life. I think that counts as a team effort."

Dorian tilted his head and thought about it for a second before nodding. "Sure, I'll allow that."

"How fucking gracious of you. Now, send the message out to the Hammers, and we can get started."

"Done. Blitz already sent a message back saying that you might want to head over to their ship. As it turns out, we got a message from the Over-Keeper too, looking to meet with us there too."

"That...doesn't bode well," Chill whispered, shaking her head. It might be a coincidence, and the Over-Keeper just wanted to run a quick update past them and the new mercs.

Not a good chance, but it was possible.

"Get ready," Chill murmured as they headed out. "Maybe the Over-Keeper found out and has a mind to rid himself of our troublesome asses once and for all."

"You think he'd be able to turn the Hammers against us?" Ivan asked. She didn't need to tell *him* to be ready. Ivan's knives would be the first weapons out.

As they approached the Hammers' ship, she saw the Over-Keeper standing with the group. He looked like someone had pissed in his squid-ink porridge when he caught sight of them.

"He looks annoyed," Kortez commented. "You think it's because—"

"Yep," Chill growled. Being attacked by the Scourge required more psychological preparation, but it was unpleasant to deal with the Over-Keeper when he was in a bad mood. She wondered if they should stop dealing with him. They would come away with fewer creds than if they stayed, but they could expose what the Jindahin were doing on the station, which would put a stop to their efforts.

It would also mean they would never be able to work as mercs again. Not having to deal with the threats and dangers that entailed was a plus, but they would have to get creative with their income stream. There was good money in security consulting, and failing that, they could make a go of it by putting their efforts into their channel.

They could try new gaming and training sims for money and put the content up since they were a credible group that had been in combat situations. That, plus the creds they would make for the interviews that fucked the Jindahin out of their secret prize, would give them a decent living.

It was something to think about if they ever got to their breaking point. It wasn't going to be an easy way to make a living, and Chill assumed there would be plenty of people looking to kill them for blabbing, but it couldn't be any less dangerous than what they were currently dealing with.

"I know what you're going to say," Blitz whispered, sidling up beside the group as they approached. "I didn't say a word. From what I understand, Kuzratha already suspected you were hiding something from him, so he pressured my people to tell him anything we might have been keeping from him. A bit of bullying and bribery later, and the felid was out of the container."

Chill nodded. It seemed odd for him to throw his own people under the bus, but they were all in an odd situation. She wasn't going to judge him for being out of his element.

"Don't worry," she replied with a small smile. "We'll handle this."

CHAPTER ELEVEN

It wasn't that she didn't understand where Blitz and his people were coming from. They were new to the station and not sure who they could trust and where they could find security while they dealt with the Scourge.

Since Kuzratha was paying them, she understood why they had turned to him for guidance. It was exactly the kind of reaction he was expecting, so all the newcomers would trust him and come to him with whatever they found. It was a good way to establish an intelligence network.

But understanding didn't mean she approved. Blitz didn't control his crew. They couldn't be trusted, not by her and not by her crew. The Hammers had chosen money over the people they would be fighting alongside. Chill would remember that about them.

"You fucked me," Kuzratha hissed through his needle-like teeth, pointing a finger at Chill as they approached. "You tried to keep me out of the loop."

"Out of what loop?" Chill countered smoothly, raising

an eyebrow. "Do you want us to fill you in on every last bit of code we manage to mine from the nests? No, we just finished decoding the data and found a point where there might be some kind of arch-nest for us to strike. We were just coming to you with this intel when we got your message."

"Bullshit!" Kuzratha snapped. "You found something to do with Lugosh's treasure, and you kept it to yourselves."

"I thought there was no such thing." She tilted her head. "Legends, rumors, nothing for us to be concerned about. We're more concerned with putting an end to the Scourge assholes out there. Chasing legends is what happens when we don't have a horde of angry bots on our tail. I mean, yeah, we heard it was a possibility from the deckies, and I'll admit it occurred to me that there might be some fact to all the fiction about the Lugosh treasure. It never occurred to me that you would want us to waste your time with that nonsense."

The Jindahin's mouth snapped shut when he realized he'd shared more than he'd intended to. Chill wouldn't give him shit for that, but if he was going to keep being a pain, she wanted him to be uncomfortable in his dealings with them.

He quickly regained his composure, though. Chill saw him activate a privacy device in his pocket, isolating them in a small bubble from which the other Hammers would not be able to listen in. Blitz was inside the bubble and could hear every word. Maybe Kuzratha had decided that he couldn't keep his plans for the station a secret from the new mercs.

"You do realize this operation still depends on me operating as the liaison with the Jindahin remnant looking to settle the area? In mercenary matters, you are in charge, but in the matters regarding the fate of the station and its future, I have the final say."

Blitz narrowed his eyes. Neither he nor the other Hammers knew about the Over-Keeper's ultimate plans. "What the hell are you talking about?" he whispered. Chill assumed he hadn't seen the privacy device go on. "Settling? Fate of the station?"

"I was under the impression that the Dead Evil team briefed you on the matter," Kuzratha muttered.

"Didn't think it was our business to talk about your plans to anyone who sauntered through the docks. No offense." Chill nodded at Blitz. "If you want the mercs to know what they're clearing the station for and what you're paying them for, you're going to have to take that leap yourself, Over-Keeper."

Wayfarers didn't have titles like that. Chill knew that, Kuzratha knew it, and Blitz probably knew it as well. Still, the Over-Keeper spilled it. All she was doing was confirming it.

"Very well." He ran his long, delicate fingers over the shimmering fabric of his shirt before nodding firmly. "I am not a Wayfarer of the Dahin. I represent a Jindahin effort to reclaim the Suneater as well as the systems it acts as a portal for inside the nebula. The station is a prize as well, which is why the Jindahin are investing a great many resources into reclaiming it."

"Why all the secrecy?" Blitz asked.

Chill shook her head. "Unless you want a nice long

education on the intricacies of Dahin politics, ask him for the short version."

"Of course."

Kuzratha was glaring at her. For the longest time, Chill had not thought the Dahin were an intimidating species. They were said to be very aggressive and powerful underwater, but they had an oddness to them on land that made them unsettling at the very worst. The Trang, Xi and Xo, ranked higher on her list because they could peek into her mind.

She'd heard horror stories about what the Xi could do when they got a lock on someone's brain.

Still, after what she'd seen the Janissaries do when they were out of their suits, the Dahin now intimidated her. Chill could feel those thin teeth sinking into her neck and tearing a chunk out of it. She'd kill him as he did it, but it was annoying that humans only had tiny, boring, blunt white bones. Nothing interesting about them.

Blitz faced her. "You've kept that information a secret as well. You've been working with this asshole the whole time, even going so far as to draw mercs in to help. Acting like you're friends with the deckies as well, all the while planning on fucking them over with whatever the Jindahin want with the station. You do realize that what he's planning will effectively be an end to their way of life?"

"A way of life that came about because they scavenge what my people left behind," Kuzratha reminded him. "All we are doing is taking back what our ancestors built."

"I knew *you* had an agenda that fucked us," Blitz snapped. "But how the hell does the DEMC justify their part in all this?"

Chill nodded. "You have no reason to believe me, but we didn't know there were people here before we came. We didn't know about the Scourge, and we sure as fuck didn't know about any treasure. Hell, we didn't even know this station existed before the Over-Keeper came to us with the job, so we had to trust him when he said he was sharing everything he knew. Since we arrived, things have changed, and there hasn't been time for us to make decisions about the future. Truth is, we assumed we would have to clear the Scourge off the station before anything *could* be decided."

"That doesn't help. We can't know if you are telling the truth." Blitz scowled.

"That's a call you'll have to make." She crossed her arms. "*We* now know that all it takes is Kuzratha asking pointed questions for your people to fold on us, so I think we can all agree that none of us trusts each other."

That was unfair, but the days of beating around the bush were behind them. The Hammers *had* handed intelligence to someone they knew couldn't be trusted. Blitz was right to call their intentions into question, but they could turn it back on him.

"We will *not* be able to retake this station with everyone looking for a dagger in the back," Chill continued. "So, Blitz, you need to have a frank and honest conversation with your crew about what you're going to do next and how we'll move forward, if at all."

"Haven't they heard everything that's been said?"

The Jindahin pulled the privacy device out of his pocket. "No, but do feel free to inform them."

"I will." Blitz bowed his head and headed to his group, which was waiting for an explanation.

"While we are rebuilding trust," Kuzratha continued after the Hammer leader was outside of the bubble, "I suppose I should tell you why I am so interested in any data regarding Lugosh and what he did on this station. I was trying to keep it a secret, but you have found me out."

"It wasn't that difficult, considering you've been pushing us for any logistical and locational data we find," Chill pointed out.

"Indeed. As it happens, Lugosh and I share a family tree. My interest in his comings and goings on the station is a deeply personal one, and it is why I was chosen to lead this enterprise. The Jindahin Elevated Court thought it would ensure I put all my time and effort into recovering the station."

"You're not going to say you have a right to claim Lugosh's treasure because he was your great-great-grand uncle twice removed on your mother's side, are you?" Kortez raised an eyebrow.

"Of course not. Well, maybe. It's more complex than laying claim." Kuzratha rolled his eyes. "Most of his 'treasure' was stolen, so it would take a lot more than just saying it's all mine. The point was never the wealth as much as the notoriety and the prestige arising from it. I will split the treasure with you as long as I can claim to have led the group that found it."

Chill sighed. It was a lot to take in. He was trying to whitewash his accusations about their trustworthiness, and promising they would all profit from the enterprise was suspicious.

But she wasn't in a position to make enemies. Henceforth, they would be expecting him to stab them in the back, but if he was meeting with them instead of the Hammers or the Harvest, his list of allies was short.

Or so she assumed. For all they knew, he'd confided his plans to all the crews and told them all they were the only ones who knew what he was really up to.

Chill looked at her crew, and it seemed as though they were all on the same page. If they weren't, she would explain it to them on the ship. They knew better than to question her decisions in front of someone they didn't trust.

"All right," she conceded with a deep sigh. "But you're going to have to stop acting like we're not in this together. If we're putting our lives on the line—all of us—we'd better fucking be doing it with all the intelligence available."

"Agreed."

"And in that regard, I thought you should see the new data." Chill pulled a tablet from inside her coat and handed it to him. It contained the work Dorian had done with Alex to clear up the mess of coding they'd collected from the nests. "As you can see, it's not the complete picture we were hoping for, but it looks like the Scourge has been trying to track it all down as well."

"What is this highlighted marker?"

"That's what we came to talk about," Chill admitted. "Since the Scourge is keeping tabs on it, chances are we are looking at one of the central nests. The number of power nodes running through the area confirms that in my mind, but we're only going to find out if we take a closer look. Close enough to blow up whatever is guarding that nest."

They had to assume there would be defenses like that massive creature from the other day in place at this one to hold them off.

"This is the only location you have?" the Over-Keeper asked. "What about all these other markers?"

"Hard to tell what they are." Chill shrugged, eyeing the rest of her crew to make sure they didn't join the conversation. "The data we have isn't complete. It would take hours or days to explore those areas, assuming there's anything to find there and it hasn't been moved. Best to work on the intelligence we have and hope the other half of this enigma is in that nest."

"I see. How do you think you will be able to approach the nest? Even with the support of the deckies, my Janissaries, and the new arrivals, it will not be easy to approach a construct like that."

Chill shook her head. "The Hammers have been working with Dorian to come up with signal codes that should render us invisible to the automated defense systems. Considering that we're heading into territory the deckies haven't visited for generations, it's practically a blank spot on the map that we'll be taking our ship to. But I think you're missing the real question."

Kuzratha tilted his head. "And that is?"

"Why the hell is the Scourge trying to track your ancestor's treasure?" Chill gave him a mirthless smile. "Odd for an AI to care about treasure. Something to keep in mind."

CHAPTER TWELVE

"Are we sure we want to do this?" Dorian was preparing for their departure.

Chill raised an eyebrow. "You're going to have to be a lot more specific." She joined him in the checks, making sure they had everything they needed to head out. "I've come up with a lot of bad ideas lately."

Dorian grinned. "Honestly, given the shit we've been dealing with, I'm surprised you haven't dropped us into a nest of cosmo-chiros yet. Until that or something just as bad happens, we're your side when it comes to what we're doing here."

"First, space bats are a myth," Chill pointed out. "No mammal can survive in a vacuum. Hell, nothing large enough to fly around in space could survive."

"Nothing we know of." Dorian tapped his temple like he was making a point. "The universe is a big fucking place. Big enough for there to be impossible shit out there."

"The universe might be big, but until we figure out a way to get to the Andromeda galaxy, I am comfortable accepting our knowledge of this galaxy as complete until proven otherwise. No point in inventing monsters in the black to worry about if we don't *know* if they exist."

He narrowed his eyes like he didn't agree with her, but she didn't need to convince him. They were talking about myths and legends nobody believed in.

"You know what?" Dorian tapped his tablet, confirming that he really did want to start the ship. "I *do* blame you. For everything. Even for Kortez having given birth to an alien. All your fault. Your punishment will be decided on by a jury of your peers."

"Don't be ridiculous." Chill grinned and hit the two-way confirmation when she felt the ship's engines rumble. "I have no peers."

"Arrogance. Typical."

She offered him her middle finger as she started the pre-flight checklist.

Chill did like having a ship of their own. It had been a good investment, offering them not only transportation but also housing and privacy. They wouldn't have had that if they had to share bunks with a bunch of other merc companies.

She would name the ship soon, assuming they still had it when a name came to her. For now, it would have to tolerate the generic name it had been given the first time they docked at an official port. It was a series of numbers, letters, and markers from a variety of languages. She recognized it on the screen, but if someone asked her for the name, she couldn't tell them.

The first five symbols were all she'd committed to

memory, and they were all she had needed so far. The people running the docks hadn't asked.

"I still don't think it's a good idea to head into the field with Kuzratha and his Janissaries," Dorian pointed out, bringing them back to the topic at hand.

"It's only two of them," Chill pointed out. "Their captain and the rest of the group are staying behind."

"But the asshole is coming with us. I like the idea of you having backup, but you have to admit that leaving him on the ship with me is going to be incredibly uncomfortable. You just know he's going to want to stay in touch with you and the team, and he's going to be pushing to make sure none of you are hiding anything from him."

He made a good point on that front, and Chill didn't like it any more than he did. She and Kuzratha had discussed it when he suggested he go with them, and they'd agreed that they needed to work on the trust thing. They were still expecting to get a dagger in their backs in the immediate future. However, since they were playing a game of politics with the mercs and the deckies at the same time, it was a good idea to pretend they were willing to trust the Over-Keeper. He would reveal his real intentions soon enough.

"Looks like we're heading into an area of the station where the defenses are still active," Dorian muttered as they got a targeting alert on their screens. "You think the Scourge is controlling those or is it automated?"

"Good question," she answered, warming their plasma cannons up as well as loading the torpedo bays. "My guess is it's automated. If the Scourge had control of the defenses, they would be a lot more aggressive and a hell of a lot more effective. Besides, we would see nests on and around the defense network platforms."

"Why?" Dorian turned to her, not focusing on where they were flying. "I mean, it might not understand that people coming from the outside might prove to be a threat, but you'd think it would have learned over the decades."

Chill shrugged. He was on a roll today, asking all the interesting questions. "Might be it's not smart enough. My guess is it's programmed not to attack anything approaching the station since it won't risk attacking its resupply sources. Which, as it turns out, we are, even though we're not here to resupply them. When we die, it will collect our ship, our suits, and our equipment and introduces it all into its cycle. Therefore, stopping us before our precious goods are safely on board would be detrimental.

"That's not to say I think the Scourge put that much thought into the situation, but it doesn't matter. The result is the same."

"You don't think it would, like, recyc our bodies, do you?" Dorian drifted the ship away from the station as more fire was sent their way. "I don't understand why an AI would have any need for organic materials."

"That depends."

"On?"

"How disturbed you want to be by the answer."

He gaped at her, neglecting his controls, but turned back when they drifted toward the tendrils of the nebula, which seemed to be reaching out at them. That wasn't a pleasant sight, but Chill wasn't comfortable with the other topic. The answer had occurred to her several days after they reached the station.

"I mean, nothing you say could be worse than what I'm thinking," Dorian suggested.

"Okay. It wouldn't take much time or effort to break our bodies down into something the Scourge could use. Beyond that, we already know that it has access to the DNA sequences of a variety of animals."

"Wait, when did we learn that?"

"Remember those number and letter sequences in the data streams?" Chill raised an eyebrow.

"Yeah?"

"Seriously, didn't you learn about genetic sequencing in school?"

Dorian shook his head. "Not really, no."

"Well, I didn't either, but I had to learn it anyway when I was a kid. I hacked into an Enterprise lab, and I wasn't sure what the hell I'd stumbled on. I needed to ask the biology professor at my school some very pointed questions while trying to keep him from wondering why I was asking."

"I suppose that makes sense." Dorian guided the ship closer to the station as more of the plasma bolts homed in on them. "And it means we now know you went to school in the Gallian Enterprise."

"The lab was Gallian," Chill cut in. "Never said I broke into it from Gallian space."

"Your defensive response confirms it."

She shrugged. "Think what you want."

"When are you going to tell us about yourself?"

Chill scowled at him. "Why would you want to know?"

"Well, if you are a serial killer who murders your crews

and uses their corpses to enact the ancient Shakespeare plays, I want to know about that shit."

That seemed reasonable. "If I told you I was not a killer with a love for old Earth plays, would you believe me?"

He considered. "I must concede that is a good point. Not the best point to make with a crew who doesn't know much about you, but a good point. I probably should have thought of it. I just don't like the idea that I might be sharing a ship with a crazy person."

"Yet you don't bring up being on the ship with Ivan. Or Kortez. If you are looking for sanity, mercenary work might not be for you."

Dorian nodded. "It's not like I chose this career path."

"Right, because petty thievery in which your victims were mercs was the sane choice." Chill shook her head. She did not want to distract the kid while he was piloting. He did have the ability to multitask. She assumed it had something to do with his genes, which had human and other races mixed in.

That wasn't a bad thing. Mixing the gene pools via interspecies copulation was a great way for the various species to leap forward.

"Everything okay up there?" Kortez called over the intercom.

"Yep," Chill replied, then looked at Dorian, who gave her a thumbs-up. "All good here. Just clearing out a couple of the surface turrets. We will arrive at the docking point closest to the arch-nest in about fifteen minutes. We don't know if there's atmo there, so stick to the appropriate protocols."

They knew what the protocols were since they'd

covered the details of what to expect in the briefing before leaving. However, it was good to remind them.

Chill should have been in the loading bay with them, but they'd decided she should manage their defenses while Dorian flew.

The plasma cannons were carving through the station's external turrets, and it didn't look like any of the larger weapons were prepped or ready to attack them. The repair functions were still working because they immediately closed up the damaged sections. They didn't repair the turrets, which were being melted off of their mounts.

They had met more resistance than they'd expected, which kept her engaged. Dorian had an intuitive way of flying, which allowed her to fire accurately even with him moving around and ahead of the shooting from the turrets.

Chill preferred to stay within a few thousand klicks of the station, even though one hit would kill them. It was preferable to facing the Scourge within, with a couple of centimeters between them and dying painfully.

"We're coming up on the dock," Dorian alerted her as Chill continued shooting. "Think we should turn our systems off to keep the Scourge from picking up on us?"

"That's one ploy," Chill muttered. "Another is to make sure we have an escape route plotted so we don't have to deal with those fucking turrets if we need to leave quickly."

If the Scourge picked up on their location early, it would be a disaster. Chill preferred to have their escape route open and ready. Chances were the Scourge was tracking their movements and they *would* need to escape.

"Approaching the dock," Dorian announced over the intercom. "Everyone get ready for...fuck, *anything*!"

"On it," Ivan replied. "We're ready to engage whatever we find in there. Janissaries are ready for action too."

Chill keyed their point defense systems. While they were useless for dealing with the attacks coming from the station, they could take out anything else they ran into.

Nothing appeared, though. Chill ran a quick scan. "I'm not picking up any bot signals in the area," she murmured. "Dorian, it looks like that airlock is pressurized. Connect us to it."

The kid nodded and redirected the ship to the airlock instead of setting it down in the docking area.

There was no telling what was hidden in the nooks and crannies of the station, which made it difficult to figure out their next move, as well as where they would be attacked from.

They preferred to have it happen in close quarters where they could control the setting. If all else failed, Ivan's explosive charges would let them beat a hasty retreat the way they'd come.

"Airlock is jammed," Ivan announced over the comm once they were connected. "Might be I could blast it open."

"Please do not set off heavy explosives in proximity to our ship," Chill interjected before he could finish his train of thought.

"I wasn't going to. Light explosives or acid to loosen everything up, not high explosives."

"Right."

"Besides, looks like the Janissaries are doing my work for me."

Chill looked at the feeds from the area. One of the Janissaries was leaning into the door. His heavy suit had enough juice to it to peel the airlock open, which caused a hiss and a rush of air as the atmo between the airlock and the station equalized.

"That was weird, right?" Dorian asked as Chill stood. "I thought these areas of the station weren't pressurized anymore."

"It was weird," she agreed. There wasn't any point in making assumptions until they knew more about the area they were stepping into.

"This whole sector is pressurized," Ivan noted as she climbed into her suit. "No toxins or problems my scanners can pick up, and atmo is holding at a solid one. Looks like something's got everything working just the way you like it."

"Yeah," Kortez chimed in. "Wouldn't want you to get space sick again."

"Whatever," Chill growled. She slotted her weapons into place before starting up the suit. Ibu had helpfully gotten everything ready for her, so all she had to do was climb in and power it on. "Are you picking up any life signs?"

"Nothing," one of the Janissaries answered. She hadn't asked him, but their suits had the better scanners. " I think you're going to want to see what we're looking at with your own eyes, though."

Chill marched through the open airlock. Thankfully, their ship was isolated from the station. Even if they weren't picking up anything, it was a good idea to make sure there was nothing in the atmo that could compromise their safety. Kortez highlighted their location on the updated map, and she joined them.

The Janissaries had fitted the Over-Keeper with a suit.

It was not like what they were wearing, but it was armor, and it looked capable of holding its own. He was carrying a caster and a sword, both intricately made and likely his personal weapons. Chill had no idea what he was doing at the front with them, but if he was willing to put his life at risk, she wouldn't argue. Dorian could thank her later.

"What the hell?" she whispered, stepping into the Vert chamber.

"Funny," the Janissary commented with a soft chortle. "That's what your buddy here said."

"I said 'what the fuck,'" Ivan corrected him. "But the point remains."

Chill wasn't sure what she was looking at. Seeing it with her own eyes wasn't helping, although she was glad to be there. The chamber had all the signs of a Scourge presence and a lot of it. Except for atmo, which was generally the first thing to go when the AI took over.

Yet, none of the Scourge in the area were active. Bots of all shapes and sizes were strewn about the place, as were their weapons and tools.

"You think this was a merc crew?" Kortez asked, approaching one of the bots.

"If it was, they didn't use casters," Ivan pointed out. He collected the carcass of one of the rat types. "Ripped apart by something pretty fucking strong."

"Not the weirdest thing we've seen mercs do." Chill shrugged as they moved farther into the chamber. "Schematics say there's a control panel in the room over there. Let's have a look at the place and see what the hell is going on."

It wasn't the kind of action they were expecting, but

Chill was coming to terms with the station twisting things for them. Not the Scourge, the station. It seemed to be alive, churning, changing, and evolving to make things more difficult for them with every step.

"All right." She highlighted defensive points around the room for the crew to take up as she settled in front of the control panel, then called up her holographic projector so they could see what she was up to.

"All right. Yeah, atmo and air scrubbers are all working to keep the area suitable for organics." Chill had seen the code before. Not the same code the Scourge used but similar, indicating they shared a source. They knew that since they'd had to deal with the coding used by the original builders of the station. The Scourge used the same sequences. "Connecting it to the day-night cycle the rest of the station is on so we can hopefully get some light..."

Her voice trailed off as the systems came online. There was no resistance to her efforts, and since everything was designed to be user-friendly, no one was surprised the station helped them get everything going.

That wasn't the surprising part of their situation.

"Are those... They can't be." Kortez shook his head.

"Not much in the galaxy looks like that," Chill answered.

"Plants? Here?" Ivan scowled. "Why would they have plants on the station?"

"Long-haul ships and stations used to grow their own food and used plants as an oxygen farm," Chill pointed out.

"Sure, a couple millennia ago." One of the Janissaries punched commands into the console, calling up a feed on the growing things. "Back when there were no Sidespace lanes and the only safe way to travel long distances was with the sub-light engines and short jumps. This station was built five hundred years after the last space-farm ship hit the decom pile. They wouldn't be included in a Jindahin station. It's primitive."

"And yet, I'm looking at plants growing in space." Chill pointed at the feed. " They're darker than the plants you usually see, although... Do any of you know anything about plants?"

Ivan shrugged. "Took a class or two back in the day. If you are thinking about the color, it might be a necessary adaptation. They need more chlorophyll with the reduced lighting, maybe? Although if they had oxygen farms on the station, you'd think they would build in windows to give them sunlight. Plenty of that in the system."

He had a point. There was no benefit in wasting resources to light the plants if they could just put in windows to take in the light from three different stars. Since there were no windows in the station, the Janissary was right. They were dealing with a foreign intruder.

Chill copied the data onto a fob and sent it to Dorian for inspection before erasing everything from the drives. "Come on. I want to get a closer look at those things."

"Are you sure that's a good idea?" Dorian countered over the comm. "I mean, there's a bunch of something ugly in there, and you're going to rush in and see what it is? Maybe poke it with a stick?"

"No sticks out here, young one," Chill answered. "I'm pretty sure Kortez would poke it with his Cortador if it acted up, though."

That got a chuckle from Kortez and Ivan, although the

Janissaries were not amused. It would take quite a bit of work to crack their thick skins, but Chill believed she would get them yet.

As more lights came on, she saw plants all around them. They were growing through the cracks or creating their own, yet they all conformed to the shapes and structures of the station. It was like they were trying to rebuild the station with organics instead of metal and prefab.

"If this infestation is aggressive, it will have to be dealt with before the Jindahin can take over the station," a Janissary pointed out.

"There's always that option." Chill approached a clump, and when she nudged it with her rifle, it felt like a plant. "Then again, given what we're seeing, it might be one of those 'enemy of my enemy' situations. Didn't have much trouble ripping the Scourge to pieces."

The soldier had no answer for that. Chill doubted anything on the station was going to be that simple, though. If these plants were fighting the Scourge, they might see the Jindahin and anyone else who came into this section as a similar incursion that needed to be eradicated.

"Got movement on the far side!" Kortez announced, highlighting the spot. "That…are those life forms?"

It seemed impossible, but the sensors were telling them it was true. They would have to run in-depth scans to be sure.

"I thought I'd seen it all when it came to this place," Chill whispered, motioning for them to take up a battle formation.

A spearhead seemed optimal. If they rushed into the thick of it, those who had the better weapons and armor should take the lead. The Janissaries didn't complain about being put up front. They were probably used to it. With Chill, Ivan, and Kortez backing them up, they could put a dent into whatever they found. The Over-Keeper was in the center of the group so the others could shield him from hostilities.

He was silent as they continued through the station, exploring their way through the area.

The Janissary leading the charge raised a fist to bring their group to a halt, then motioned for them to take up defensive positions. They had come to an open courtyard within a circle of buildings around a crumbling fountain.

They no longer needed to question whether the Scourge had tried to push in after its original defeat. The familiar rat and felid bots were picking their way through the foliage, and the plants were grabbing the bots.

Most interesting, the bots were not reacting to the growth. They were ignoring the plants, which pushed up out of the cracks and crevices they were hiding in to secure the bots.

The bots didn't look at the plants that grabbed at them, although they tried to pull free. Otherwise, they made no effort to dislodge the plants.

"That's weird," Chill whispered as she recorded their interactions. "Never thought I would see the Scourge fail to react to something like it owed them creds."

None of them understood what they were looking at, neither from the perspective of the bots or the plants. The plants weren't very strong, so the bots could eventually free themselves and continue walking.

Odder, the plants weren't attempting to do the same to

the newcomers, and that wasn't the end of the surprises. There was movement all around them.

Creatures, this time. Chill had never seen anything like the powerful-looking bipeds who stooped under the weight of their pale bodies. The dark plants growing inside them indicated which side they were on.

They were carrying crude weapons fashioned from pieces of sharp metal or other scavenged materials.

"We've found out how the Scourge creatures were torn to pieces," the Over-Keeper commented. "What are they?"

"Fuck if I know," Ivan whispered. "But it doesn't look like they're friendlies, whatever the hell they are."

As if to prove his point, a dozen of the bipeds attacked the Scourge bots, which were still trying to pick their way clear of the plants and foliage.

The beasts enthusiastically tore into the bots before they could react, using their improvised weapons to pry them apart.

"Oh. We've stumbled into an interesting situation." Chill inched back on instinct. She wasn't sure why, but then her screen filled with Scourge readings.

It was a trap. A simple one, but effective. The Scourge had drawn the bipeds out with the kinds of creatures they were expecting before sending the shock troops in.

There were enough to pose a threat, even to people who had nothing to do with the fighting.

"We should get out of here," Chill whispered. "Not that I don't want to collect more data on these creatures, but it looks like things are going to get dicey."

"No," the Over-Keeper cut in. "We've come this far. Let

the Scourge fight it out with the creatures. We can circle around them and keep moving toward the map marker."

It was too late for Chill's suggestion anyway. The Scourge was coming from all sides, but the plant-infected creatures were putting up a good fight.

It wasn't going to last long, though. Reinforcements for both sides appeared, then the plant creatures retreated the way they'd come, hacking at the bots in their path. The Scourge rushed in to cut them off, tearing up plants as they attacked.

Confirming that the Scourge could set traps and draw an enemy out of hiding was disturbing.

With that in mind, Chill directed their group down the path the Janissaries had highlighted. It was empty of bots, but that wouldn't last. She'd fought enough of them to know that.

"Ivan, you got anything for me?" Chill shouted as they picked up speed.

"Always," he answered. He pulled a handful of grenades out of his pack and tossed her a couple. Chill was proud when she caught the grenades without breaking stride.

She primed the first of them, noting the points where the bots had bunched up. They didn't want to involve themselves in the fighting, but if the fighting came to them, she wanted to make a big splash.

She wanted to avoid damaging the plant-infected bipeds. Chill didn't want to jeopardize their chance to work with them by accidentally blowing them up.

"They've spotted us!" Ivan shouted, indicating a group of bots who had turned away from their attack on the plants to focus on the newcomers.

Chill primed one of the grenades and tossed it smoothly across the atrium before the Scourge could attack. The throw was helped by a lucky bounce off a nearby wall, and it landed in the middle of the bots.

A wet pop resulted in most of the creatures disintegrating or turning to shrapnel that wrecked more of the creatures. They now had the full attention of the Scourge.

Most of the bots had turned away from their assault on the greenery and focused on the humans and the Dahin. The group had the attention of the plant creatures too. The bipeds seemed confused by their presence, and they made no move to help or hinder them.

Another element Suneater Station had thrown at them. Chill didn't like how high the pile was getting.

"Keep moving!" she roared, waving them forward as she opened fire on the Scourge bots that were running at them. More came out of the walls. They had a whole horde coming at them.

She paused to look for the map marker. They couldn't run away from the Scourge. Eventually, they would have to fight, and she wanted to do that in a location where they had the advantage. Otherwise, they would be funneled to where the Scourge had the advantage.

Chill dropped two of the grenades, having set them to go off when a bot got close. She opened fire on the rest, cutting into their lines. They hissed and spat as they surged forward.

She wasn't sure why she was trying to hold them off. The others were firing and setting traps to slow the things down, but they couldn't hold the Scourge off in their current location. The bots could come at them from all sides.

"Boss, we have a problem!" Kortez shouted. She returned her attention to her group, which had skidded to a halt in front of a massive door.

The schematics showed it as being open, which was clearly not true.

"We need to bust through the door," Chill told Ivan, who was more than happy to oblige her. He reached into his pouch and extracted some boom powder.

"No!" Kuzratha had a panicked note in his voice as he stepped in front of Ivan to keep him from blowing the door. "There is another way."

"Not according to our schematics, there isn't," Chill countered as she fired at a felid that had gotten past her grenades without setting them off.

The rats behind set the felid set the grenades off and cleared the area for them.

"The schematics are obviously incomplete." The Over-Keeper scowled at her, then moved to the wall near the door and pressed a handful of nearby levers. She'd seen those all over the place and never thought anything of them. She'd assumed the circuits had worn out or something else had broken, rendering them useless.

Not in this case. When he pressed the third lever, a clunk loud enough to be heard through the shooting and explosives echoed through the chamber, and a smaller door opened.

Not small*er*. It was short and narrow. Chill wasn't sure her team could use it, and the Janissaries couldn't in their heavy suits.

"You'll need to get out of them." She made the call when Kuzratha went through the door, not waiting for them to scan what was waiting for him. The Over-Keeper had decided that whatever was there could not be worse than what was coming at them on this side.

The Janissaries exchanged looks. It couldn't be an easy decision for the Dahin, considering they had sworn oaths to retain their weapons and armor in the presence of outsiders.

She couldn't force them to take the suits off, but she could guarantee that if they didn't, they would be left behind to deal with the Scourge on their own. They would be killed.

They would make the decision without any intervention from her besides the suggestion she'd already offered.

"Right." One of them peeled his chest plate back, and the suit opened. He climbed out, collected a sidearm and a rifle, and went through the door.

His comrade hesitated, then he too climbed out of his suit and selected weapons to carry before moving through.

Chill stepped through next. She had to turn sideways and duck to make it. It was more challenging for Kortez, who crouched and shuffled sideways to get through. Ivan was comfortable with the tight space and overtook them before the door closed behind them.

It wouldn't keep the Scourge off their backs for long, but it was comforting to have a wall between them and the bots.

If there wasn't anything worse on this side.

CHAPTER THIRTEEN

Chill wasn't sure what she'd expected. Piles of gold and jewels? That wasn't what they found.

They walked into an antechamber with tasteful lighting and interesting sculptures and paintings. A person with a passion for the arts had set the room up.

"You think those paintings are the treasure?" Kortez suggested, nudging Chill gently in the ribs. Well, he tried to be gentle, but due to his suit, the playful gesture almost knocked her over. "Oh, sorry."

"No problem," she answered, carefully adjusting her balance with some help from the suit. "Why would the paintings be the treasure?"

"I don't know. They look old and well-done, which means they'll be worth something to someone. They'll be worth a lot more to people who want to get their hands on relics from the old Suneater station."

"I guess that *is* possible," she conceded as she approached one of the paintings. "Not a lot of people know much about the Serpent, but those who do would probably drop two or three mil on pieces like these. Not retirement-level creds, and that's what people tend to think of when you say 'treasure,' but not an amount to be scoffed at either."

"These pieces are considerably more valuable than that," Kuzratha murmured, approaching another of the pieces. "These are hundreds of years old and came from all over the galaxy. People have been looking for these for centuries, assuming they were in some rich person's private collection. Just one of these would fetch hundreds of millions of creds, assuming you could find the right buyer."

Chill was tempted. The pieces were old and fragile, so she would have to be delicate in her handling. They wouldn't be able to take any of the paintings through the horde of monsters waiting for them outside.

Still, hundreds of millions of creds was the kind of fortune people like her hoped to score. Most of them never did, but when one just dropped on their laps, it would be a waste not to take advantage.

One of the smaller pieces. No need to be greedy. The Over-Keeper likely thought all the pieces belonged to him, but he *had* said he would be willing to share the treasure if he got the credit for finding it.

"Please do not touch the *objets d'art.*" The voice came from behind her. Chill realized she had been inches away from grabbing the nearest one. Everyone else was looking at her, and she felt self-conscious. Still, it wasn't like they weren't all thinking the same thing. She had never been one to obsess about art. Paint on canvas was all it was to her—and a hefty paycheck if sold to someone who did care.

The voice had come up from a holographic projection that had popped up when she'd gotten too close, likely an automatic butler to ensure that people didn't ruin the pieces. He probably had not made an appearance for a while, although the lack of dust in the room was interesting to note. There were automated cleaning and preservation programs in place to make sure that while the *objets*, as he'd called them, were old, they were maintained in pristine condition.

The Dahin—no surprise there—was decked out in the finery his people were known for, although his clothing was outdated, or so it seemed to Chill.

Not outdated, she realized after studying the intricate hologram. It was a naval uniform from an earlier time, but the rank insignia was unmistakable.

"Greetings, and welcome to the antechamber for Captain Lugosh's private collection."

That sounded like an AI's programmed greeting. It had little meaning, but it was light and pleasant and would set anyone who heard the voice—who hadn't been chased through the doors by murderous robots—at ease.

Ivan nudged her shoulder and pointed out the pipes in the room, which started at the pillars and ran up to the ceiling. "It's an energy loop. Light engines feed it power that runs through the pipes, using the fluid they carry—a super-heavy element—as a liquid-state drive. I've only heard stories about people pulling that shit off. It must be what's running the AI."

It seemed rude to be discussing the AI like it wasn't

standing there, studying them with an expression of bemusement. It had probably been based on Lugosh.

"Identify," Kuzratha stated, approaching the hologram.

The AI raised a hand in what looked like a greeting, but it emitted bursts of light as it collected data on the Dahin in front of him.

"Welcome, Over-Keeper Barr'Nas Kuzratha." It bowed its head in deference. "Recognized as a direct descendant of Captain Lugosh. Full access to the vault has been granted."

"Huh." Chill tilted her head as she approached the holographic image. "I'm going to try something. Identify."

The AI turned to her and ran the same scan. It adopted the bemused expression again when the scan was over.

"Apologies. Your identity could not be verified. Authorized personnel may invite you into the restricted sections of the vault. Entering without authorization will incur penalties."

"What sort of penalties?" Kortez asked, crossing his arms.

"Authorized personnel may invite you into the restricted sections of the vault," the AI repeated. "Entering without authorization will incur penalties."

"I think we're going to need to wait for the Over-Keeper to invite us," Ivan suggested. "I would not like to incur those penalties."

"Your understanding is appreciated." The AI smiled.

"Oh, fuck, that's creepy," Chill muttered. "So, what...is that the visage of your long-dead...uncle, or whatever?"

"No." Kuzratha shook his head. "He must have been based on the memories and intentions of one of Lugosh's most faithful officers to keep his treasure safe."

"That is correct," the AI asserted. "My visage, demeanor, voice, and intentions were based on Corporal Seni'Tai Morsha. I maintain the physical remains of the life and times of Lugosh."

"I don't even want to know how all that was extracted from someone's mind," Ivan muttered. "I thought cerebral cortex mapping was made illegal after people found out what the long-term effects were on the mind of the subject. Well, I say 'subject.' What I mean is 'victim.'"

"The fucker was a pirate," Chill reminded him. "I doubt something like sentients' rights would keep him from doing whatever the fuck he wanted to. Besides, this corporal probably volunteered for the job. Talk about a way to live forever. In theory, anyway."

"Still." Kortez shook his head. "Maintaining a treasure like the art pieces in this gallery seems like work for a regular-ass AI. Hell, a VI could probably do the job for a fraction of the power demand. It's a waste to set up this incredibly complex, power-hungry, and illegal means just to look after some canvases."

"The *objets* are indeed a part of a collection Captain Lugosh intended to maintain," the AI explained. "And his treasure is not the art pieces."

"Well, no need to keep us in suspense," Chill answered, approaching the projection. "What is the treasure he's put so much time and effort into keeping hidden?"

Its face went blank. "That information is classified."

She scowled. "Classified by whom?"

"That information is classified."

"That corporal who got his brain fried for this had a

one-track mind, didn't he?" She shook her head. "Doesn't matter."

"It matters to me," Kuzratha interrupted. "What is the treasure?"

The AI smiled. "Access to classified information granted. Please ensure that anyone in earshot is authorized to be informed. For your convenience, here is a list of those who are in the room."

Chill tilted her head as data streams about them showed up in front of the Over-Keeper. Thankfully, all it appeared to know about her was her mononym and current occupation.

"Really happy it's only showing five faces," Kortez muttered. "I don't feel like having to deal with an eaves-dropper."

Kuzratha rolled his eyes and tapped the holographic button to accept that all those present were authorized to have the information.

"Thank you. Now, the treasure is revealed to all of you." It raised its hands, and the loop over their heads and in the pillars glowed a pale pearly white, showing off the essence of the liquid inside.

"The liquid-state drive is the treasure?" Ivan asked. "I mean, it's fucking unique, but I'm pretty sure we could get a better price on the *objets* than that."

"What you see is an engine powered by the liquid-state drive," the AI explained, showing annoyance at Ivan's flip-pant attitude. "The engine is powered by the liquid-state drive, and while a fraction of the power produced is devoted to maintaining my systems, its core purpose is to maintain the treasure of Lugosh."

Chill looked around, then shook her head. "Yeah, I'm going to need a lot more information than that."

The AI continued like it hadn't heard her. "The drive's power is dedicated to maintaining and circulating a Sidespace envelope bound within the station and fed by energy from the star. The treasure may only be accessed by Lugosh or his living descendants and only after the station has been secured. Only then can the Sidespace exit protocols for the contained envelope be accessed."

It was Ivan's turn to look confused. "Maintaining a Sidespace lane that small is... I don't think that's even possible."

"It is," Chill answered. "Theoretically, you could oscillate a Sidespace envelope between two points micrometers apart. The problem is that every oscillation would require the same amount of power to be recycled each time, and the shorter the distance between the two points, the faster the oscillation would be. Punching a hole like that requires massive amounts of power, but as long as you spread it over a certain distance, the engine can recycle that power. Three or four parsecs is the required distance for most commercial engines these days, although higher-grade military vessels can do it in under one. Keeping it to a distance of...what, three or four hundred thousand klicks? That would be impossible when you don't have the combined power of three suns feeding your engine."

They were all looking at her again, this time like she was an alien who had babbled a bunch of garbage that was both offensive and dirty.

"That is correct," the AI stated, breaking the silence. "Of course, warnings must be issued. The envelope was created not only as a means to keep thieves from taking the treasure but also to keep what is inside from causing havoc. Lugosh's Sidespace envelope solution was devised only after elements of his treasure escaped containment and infested portions of the ship."

"Should have seen this coming," Kortez muttered. "You're going to tell us the Scourge escaped and started tearing the station up."

"I am not going to tell you that." The AI studied Kortez for a few seconds, then turned back to Kuzratha. "I was brought into being to assist in creating a solution to effectively isolate the remaining treasure from the rest of the galaxy, as well as to protect the Serpent from the biological infestation taking hold. Captain Lugosh was in possession of many interesting and dangerous biological weapons, one of which you saw upon entering this chamber, which has been sealed against entry."

Chill shook her head again. "You're telling us the greenery out there is the result of a biological agent that was accidentally unleashed on the station? And that there are more elements like that inside the envelope Kuzie is trying to access?"

"I think you're missing the main point," Ivan whispered.

"No, I'm pretty sure I'm on the right path."

"Understanding the inherent threat in what we're trying to get our hands on is important as hell," Ivan conceded. "But this AI is the one in charge of keeping that…whatever, infestation from spreading through the entire station and taking over. What did we see fighting the infestation out there?"

It took her a few seconds to put the pieces together.

Silence fell over the room. Chill felt sick. "You're the Scourge," she whispered.

The AI paused like it was trying to address the comment. "Yes, and at the same time, very much no. It's more complicated than that."

"It seems pretty fucking simple from where I'm standing," Kortez growled.

"Then I would suggest you find another place to stand." Once again, there was that hint of annoyance in its voice. "What you call the 'Scourge' is a defensive protocol instituted to halt and eliminate the mutants and the creeping infections that come with them. If allowed to spread unchecked, the infections would compromise the integrity of the station's Verts, which would eventually collapse the station, as well as cause damage to the surrounding systems and areas of the galaxy.

"Unfortunately, in performing that element of my programming, I found that I needed to grow and adapt as the mutants did the same. Elements of the defensive protocols were left to perform their duties automatically, with code that would allow them to spread and adapt to combat the threat of infections. As the copies and copies of copies spread, there was a deterioration of their core coding that directed them to view all organic life on the station as a threat to be removed."

"So, you spread yourself too thin, and you lost control of the AI defense system you unleashed on the rest of the station?" Kuzratha offered that as a simple explanation.

"In so many words, yes. By the time I discovered that, many people had already died, and those who survived had fled. I failed to allow for the possibility of data corruption resulting in all organics being perceived as threats. There is something that can be done to correct the situation, however."

"If it's singing about a Daisy Girl, I am done with this conversation," Chill warned.

"I do not understand."

"Never mind. What is the solution?"

"A reboot is possible. I still exercise administrator control over the Scourge's nests, so I can provide you with signal coding that, when projected, will confuse or pacify the Scourge when you encounter it. If I can connect to one of the command nodes—what you call nests—I can force a reboot and restore the Scourge to its original settings and goals, minus the corruption. The Scourge, as it stands, has enough resources to eliminate the mutants in one fell swoop, but the diversification of its priorities has watered its efforts down. With the original coding restored, I can eliminate the mutants and retake the Serpent."

It sounded like a solid plan, but Chill had long ago learned that when something sounded too good to be true, it was. She didn't trust the AI since it had been responsible for creating the Scourge. The deckies would feel the same way and probably with a great deal more fervor.

Yet, it was a solution—a way to put an end to the war that would kill them all eventually.

"We need to regroup," Chill announced. "Get back to Coil Cove and gather our resources and support to hit one of the central nodes. If what you say is true, we have a shot at this, but the Scourge will fight us every step of the way. I want to make sure we can get it done."

"Sounds like a plan, boss." Kortez nodded firmly.

"Why do you believe I can lie?" the AI asked, tilting its holographic head.

"I'm not going to answer that," she stated. "Are you with us, Over-Keeper?"

The Dahin looked more subdued than he ever had in their presence before. He nodded his agreement.

CHAPTER FOURTEEN

Getting back to Coil Cove proved to be a lot easier than getting into the antechamber had been. The AI had cleared the bots out, or the plant infestation had. Nothing tried to stop them from going back to the ship with the data the Treasure Keeper had given them.

They would not know if it was a solution until they tried it in the field, but when she looked at the coding, Chill gained confidence.

It wasn't that she didn't trust the AI—although she didn't—but it was an antiquated piece of tech. As impressive as the engineering feat was, there might be weak points in its coding.

If they were going to try it, they had to do it soon.

The Over-Keeper hadn't left with the crew, preferring to stay in the antechamber. He had promised he would keep in touch with them as they headed back, but he hadn't said a word over the comm by the time they got back to Coil Cove.

Chill understood his need for contemplation. Running

into the makings of a family fortune on the station had likely been his dream since the job of reclaiming the station had been offered to him. Also, much of the treasure was a variety of weapons. If the plant infestation the Scourge had been created to stop had caused this much trouble, the weapons Kuzratha would have access to could tip the balance of the war between the Dahin factions.

The Over-Keeper would be remembered and praised for that by his people, but Chill didn't want any part in it. Neither would he want mercs to have any part in it. The Dahin would want the weapons to be the kind of secret they'd all hoped Mugh-9 would remain forever. The mercs would be prevented from revealing their information either through legal means, by paying them to sign non-disclosure agreements, or by killing them.

Considering the latter option was the cheaper and more effective option, she had a feeling it was the one they would go with.

However, they already had the data. Chill would collate it and load it onto an anonymous server to be shared with the news agencies on the caster network if they suffered any accidents. She and her crew wouldn't take being stabbed in the back lightly

For the threat to be effective, Kuzratha would have to know about it, and it wouldn't go over well.

They wouldn't tell him about it until the data was ready to be distributed. Otherwise, it would give him time to forestall their actions. She would have to figure out how to tell the Over-Keeper without giving too much away, or the Jindahin would try to wipe the data before eliminating them.

It would have to be multiple packets—at least five, stored in secure locations. She'd connect AIs or VIs to implants that tracked their life signs. They would have to be foolproof and not trigger the release if an anomaly in the galaxy interrupted the signal.

"You've got that look on your face again," Dorian noted once they'd hit open space and were speeding back to Coil Cove.

"I've been considering that we have knowledge the Jindahin Salifate might decide it wants to kill us over and figuring out how to blackmail them into paying us a bonus and leaving us alone instead."

"You want to blackmail our employer?" Dorian tilted his head. "We're stooping to that?"

"Not really blackmail. A way to keep them from trying to kill us," she answered. "We have data on the treasure, and they will want to use the weapons that are part of it in their war against their own people. They will kill us to keep it from getting out."

"You really think they would kill us to keep us quiet?"

"Have you *met* the Jindahin?" Chill raised an eyebrow.

"Sure, but we're working for them, so they should trust us."

"They don't. That's the point."

"You're assuming that."

Chill shook her head. "I've intercepted their communications. I have been for a while because you're damn straight. I *don't* trust them enough to not keep an eye on them after all we've had to put up with from them. Anyway, the Over-Keeper's higher-ups are complaining that we're not moving at the pace they want us to, and even if we're contractually engaged with them, they can just get rid of us."

"Oh. Okay. There aren't a lot of other ways for us to take that. Still, Kuzratha might not do it."

"Yeah, because if he's going to have to split his family fortune with a bunch of mercs he doesn't even like, why *wouldn't* he keep us around?" Chill shrugged. "When it comes time to decide whether there's a benefit to leaving us alive versus killing us off, he'll pick the easier option. We need to tip the scales toward benefit so he'll keep us around or let us go on our way. Hell, if we play this right, we might end up incredibly rich and with the Jindahin working very hard to keep us from getting killed."

"You really think that's how it's going to play out?"

"Fuck, no. If anything, they'll spill all the beans themselves and deny everything, *then* go after us."

"Yeah, that sounds about right. But it is fun to imagine."

Chill wasn't paying attention. The merc crews and the deckies were exchanging hostile communications. She shouldn't tap into the communications of their allies, but they'd tried to fuck her over before, and she wasn't going to let it happen again.

Alex kept track of the conversations, and when there was something alarming, she brought Chill into the loop. They also had a marker for when people started speaking in what appeared to be code.

They were in the middle of nowhere in space, and just about everything was trying to kill them. While it would piss people off if they knew, she risked it to keep her crew alive and out of the worst of the danger.

"What's going on?" Dorian asked, picking up on what she was looking at.

"There's been some shit going on in our absence," Chill answered, calling up the communications. "Fighting too. The Hammers sided with the Harvest, and the more disgruntled members of the decky crews are planning to go after the arch-nest to wreck it themselves. Looks like they have aspirations to take over the Serpent and get rid of the Jindahin remnants who might stop them.

"Not all of the decky crews are on board, though. Shoviil is still pulling the strings when it comes to the groups. He's convincing them that they will have a place in the new order, and it will be better than the marginal life they were living before we got there. He's laying it on a little thick, but it appears to be working."

"If you mean they will be looking for a way to kill us all when we get back, he's doing a great job."

It was good to know they would just run into the jaws of a trap. The Sempers didn't have the pull they used to, but it wouldn't take a lot of convincing for them to end up in a fight for their lives. The Janissaries could hold their own until the rest of their people got back.

"We should let the Over-Keeper know about this," she whispered, tapping buttons on the tablet. She told Kuzratha what would be waiting for them when they got back. Part of her reason for sending the message was to find out if he was keeping tabs on communications too.

"Is this correct?" the Over-Keeper asked over the comm a few seconds after she transmitted the data.

"From what Shoviil's been telling me, yes."

"You're sure he can be trusted?"

"Well, he hasn't tried to fuck anyone over yet. I mean, he did try to kill us when we first met, but you'd be surprised how often that happens. I've learned not to take it personally."

"We're going to have to work through the infighting if we want to take the station back," Chill continued.

"Not anymore," Kuzratha muttered over the comm, sounding like he was lost in thought. "If the Treasure Keeper is right, all we need is to get into the arch-nest, and the Scourge will work for us instead. Then we won't need to worry about any of this."

"You wouldn't have found that out if it wasn't for the deckies," Chill countered smoothly. "If you put all the people who helped you out to pasture, nobody will be willing to work for you in the future."

The threat was less veiled than she'd intended. She hoped it got the point across that they weren't going to let him screw over the people who were helping him.

"I'm going to look at what we're going into," Chill announced, turning the comm off before the Over-Keeper could reply. "Are the sensors we set up on the dock working?"

"They are," Alex assured her. "Unfortunately, they are useless in our current situation since they are set to trigger in the presence of Scourge bots. You would have to reset them manually to look for anything else."

"A simple no would have sufficed," she muttered. "Kortez, Ivan, we're going in blind. Get ready for a hostile reception."

"Already on it, boss," Kortez answered. "Are you joining us?"

Chill turned to Dorian, who waved her away.

"We cleared most of the turrets out of this sector. I should be good," he told her. "Go get ready to fight with the crew. You know you want to."

She did want to, and she hadn't needed to fire on turrets on the way back. Sticking to the cockpit would be a waste of time. If Dorian needed help, Alex could do it.

"So, looks like we're heading into a mess," Ivan commented when she got down to the loading bay. "I don't suppose we could have done anything to prevent it?"

"Probably, but I'll hold off on the hindsight until I know more about the situation." Chill climbed smoothly into her suit, powered it up, and commed Kuzratha. "Shoviil is organizing the friendlies, but considering how many are against them, he's in for a fight, even with the Janissaries on their side. They *will* be on their side, right?"

The question was directed to the Over-Keeper. "Of course. If the situation is as bad as your man says it is, they will likely focus their aggressive efforts on my people first."

Shoviil wasn't her man, but there was no point in correcting him. The Xo's crew was gone, and Chill looked out for him.

"It should be an interesting fight," Kortez muttered. "Didn't think we would be pitting ourselves against those Hammers. Not this soon, anyway. I was starting to like those bastards."

Chill grinned. "I mean, at some point, we would have to fight them anyway. Mercs don't get to choose who they fight. In this case, they did, and they chose us."

"What about the Harvest?" Ivan asked, raising an

eyebrow. "New arrivals. I didn't think we would be at odds with them."

"So soon," Kortez countered, settling into his suit. "I assumed we would end up fighting them, if only because of how they made their appearance."

Chill couldn't argue with his logic. The Harvest crew had made a mess of the situation by shooting at whatever crossed their path when they'd arrived. They hadn't done anything to change anyone's perception of them or the Harvest. She didn't know much about the group aside from the rumors, but it was apparent that the group had started those rumors, intentionally or not.

"We're going to demonstrate that it was a mistake to fuck with us," she said with a grin. "While the Harvest doesn't know how problematic we are, the Hammers do. We'll show them the error of their ways and remind them why DEMC is one of the most feared outfits in the galaxy. I might be patting my own back here, but we've done a great deal of work to make it so people don't underestimate us."

No one spoke for a moment. She could hear the soft clacks of their suits as they moved around.

"You're getting better at this speech business, boss," Zichix commented, his eyes making it look like he was smiling.

"Yep," Kortez agreed, tapping his rifle. "Feeling right and ready for a good bout of excessive violence because of that."

"Please. You're *always* ready for excessive violence," Ivan pointed out. "But he's right. That was a good way to get us riled up and ready to go. That should be your job from now on."

"Seems like the job of a captain," Zichix pointed out.

"Yeah, yeah. The three of you can shut the fuck up." She rolled her eyes and pulled her rifle out of its holster. "Dorian, do you have eyes?"

"Oh, yeah. I've got plenty of eyes. The decky crews are committing violence against each other. I'm not picking up any sign of the Janissaries."

"The Janissaries are in and near the Over-Keeper's ship," one of them answered, reminding her that they were there. She'd almost forgotten. "There is no point in setting up anywhere else unless we want the enemy to take our ship and leave us stranded."

"That's our first move," Chill asserted. "Get the Over-Keeper's ship and take it back if necessary. Any questions?"

There were none.

"Excellent. Let's get going, then."

CHAPTER FIFTEEN

"I expected the Harvest and the Hammers to give us more of a fight," Kortez pointed out, checking his rifle again.

"There's a good reason for that," Chill answered.

"Yeah?"

"They're not here."

She'd noticed that the moment they came off the ship. She'd expected to walk into a hail of caster fire, but they had been greeted by a smattering of shots from those few who noticed they'd come back—not the welcome they'd expected. The deckies were too busy fighting between themselves to pay attention to them.

"Where the fuck did they go?" Ivan asked.

"Off to battle it out with the arch-nest and try to take over the station from their communications." She slotted her rifle back into its holster as those deckies who had been fighting with or for the Harvest lowered their weapons. "Didn't pick up that they had left, so they must have just gone."

It wasn't the best start. They needed to play catch-up, which meant finding the Janissaries and making sure Coil Cove was secure before going after the rest of them.

As it turned out, the Janissaries had holed up in the Over-Keeper's ship. Chill couldn't blame them. They were cut off from their superior, and hostilities that were outside their control had erupted, so they retreated to hold their ship. They were waiting for orders when the DEMC got to them.

That wasn't what Chill expected from Special Forces. They operated outside the usual command structure, which allowed them to make their own decisions about who to kill and why.

"Good to see you're back," the Janissary commander greeted them with a small bow. "Seems like the deckies got a mind to start some violence. Most of them were shooting at us, so we are holding the ship until orders come through."

"A sound decision." Chill smiled even though he couldn't see it through her helmet's visor. "However, the situation was caused by the mercenaries, not the deckies. They decided to avoid dealing with us and try to take the main nest on their own. They probably assumed they would be able to take the station after that."

The captain snorted derisively, a sound he probably didn't intend them to hear. "Even if they clear the Scourge out, given their numbers, they can't hope to hold the station. Not to disparage their skills, but they shouldn't have split their force up as their first move."

He had a point. Chill just hoped there was more to their

decision than taking the station. The Hammers had been around long enough to know they couldn't do it on their own. Then again, Chill didn't give anyone much credit when it came to intelligence. Their greed might have overtaken their sense.

Or it could be something else. She wouldn't know until they caught up with the mercs and she could ask them what their plans were down the barrel of a rifle.

"Chill!" Shoviil waved for a group of deckies to join him as he approached. "I am relieved to see you all here and alive. I tried to stop them; I really did. You have no idea how quickly shit went out of control. I tried to keep the people on our side organized. It wasn't going our way until the mercs and their decky followers decided they wanted to attack the fucking arch-nest on their own. You have to believe me."

"I do," she assured him, placing a suited hand on his shoulder. Considering he didn't know she had tapped into the comms, it wouldn't be a stretch for her to assume he was a part of the mutiny, if that was the word for it. He thought he had to assure his allies that he was still very much on their side.

"Unfortunately, our next step isn't any different from theirs. We have to get to the arch-nest and hopefully keep the Scourge from killing us while we're clearing the station."

"You think you'll be able to do that?"

She shrugged. "We've got a plan. If all goes well, it will end up with the Scourge reverting to its original coding and securing the station for us. Assuming not everything will go to plan, though, we still will have cleared out a massive source of the Scourge's power in the Vert."

"I-I see. You really believe the Scourge will fight for us after you tweak its software?"

"No, but that was what was promised, and I'm nothing if not an optimist. Commander, are your troops ready to move out? We're going to need all the firepower you can bring on this. We were told that fixing the software would make things easier, but we're still heading right into the thick of it."

"What about our ships?" Kharkanaw gestured at the vessels. "Do you think it's wise to leave them unguarded? They will be easy pickings for the scavengers."

"We have higher priorities to deal with than the ships, Commander," Kuzratha cut in before Chill could answer. "Retaking this station will require every last ounce of fighting power we have. For that, I am relying on your skills and experience, as well as that of Captain Chill."

"For the last time, it's just Chill," she growled.

"As you wish, Your Eminence," Kharkanaw told Kuzratha, then gestured to his men to get ready for combat.

"We're going to need all our fighting power in the field, too," Chill told Dorian over the comm. "That means taking our mechs. Well, we can leave one behind for Alex to pilot in case there's trouble on the home front."

"Don't worry about Alex handling the mech," Ibu announced over the comm. "I can handle whatever's coming our way."

"Are you—"

NEW RULES FOR INCOMPETENTS

"Sure I can handle a mech suit I've been taking apart and putting back together? Which I've been working on the sims for and practicing when I have downtime? I've got this, Chill. Just get out there and kick some serious bot ass."

"Wait, why are we leaving defenses behind when the Janissaries don't have to?" Dorian asked.

Chill shrugged. "Because we'll be flying us ahead of the mercs, and it's our best way to get back out of the heat if we need to. It'll need the defenses."

"Assuming they have asses." Kortez pulled his helmet off as their group started assembling. "Do bots have asses?"

"I mean, there *are* sexbots," Chill mused aloud. "Those designed to appeal to humans would have them, I guess. No other reason for them to have the subcutaneous padding on the rear end that humans and humanoids developed."

It wasn't something she generally thought about. Most bots were designed for utility or familiarity, but some elements were not added without a purpose. Large posteriors were a balance issue, or that was the excuse the devs gave when one was asked for. The weights added as counterbalances gave the sex bots the aesthetically pleasing hourglass shape male humanoids wanted. They also had pleasant feminine voices.

Some had desirable masculine shapes instead of feminine. Chill had been surprised to find that those were only half as popular as their more feminine counterparts, although there was a large market for them.

"Brooding?" Ivan asked.

"Not unless you can brood about why bots with large

asses and tits are more popular than the bots with massive...muscles," Chill commented. "Pretty sure that doesn't count, considering there aren't any pleasure and pleasantry bots around here. At least, none *I* would consider P&P bots. Knowing what's out there on the net, someone has a rabid killer bot fetish."

A moment later, the parties were ready to head out. No big speeches. They all knew their jobs, and they would get them done.

The Janissaries didn't look any different than they had in other fights, aside from carrying extra packs. One had a repeater set up on his shoulder, and a couple had rocket launchers. It seemed like overkill, but since they would be fighting the Scourge *and* the mercs, it probably wasn't.

They went to their ship and headed back out. Chill wished they'd had more time to plan their approach, but they wanted to beat the crews to the arch-nest and keep them from causing too much damage.

If the others wrecked the nest before the patch could be installed, they would have to find another centralized point for them to implement the coding that the Treasure Keeper had offered the Over-Keeper.

When they were in range, the ship broadcast the signal that kept the turrets from targeting the ship, treating it like a friendly approach.

Chill commented as they continued their approach, "Until we figure out what network those turrets are on, we should share this code with any ships that want to approach to keep them from being fired on."

"We will discuss it after this operation," the Over-Keeper replied. He hadn't been his usual overbearing self since they'd located his ancestor's treasure. Chill wondered if it was because he was starting to consider the dour possibilities of the treasure he was inheriting.

If there were more bio-plagues that would create aggressive foliage, Chill would decline that part of the treasure. At the same time, she didn't want to hand a weapon like that to the Jindahin since she knew the people they'd use it against.

That was a matter for later. They had been hired to clear the station, not make the Over-Keeper rich. If they were not given a choice about how those weapons would be used, they would kill Kuzratha—and likely have to fight the Janissaries, which they might not survive.

If there was no other heir to unlock the vault, the Jindahin would not be able to access the weapons. They might eventually hack their way in without triggering the inevitable swarm of countermeasures, but the DEMC could slow them down and warn the rest of the galaxy before they could do that.

There was no telling how the rest of the galaxy would take it. With her luck, the news would either be buried, or it would trigger a wave of reactions that would escalate the conflict to the point of killing millions of people across dozens of systems. Chill didn't want her decisions to enter into galactic politics, but she couldn't control that.

Chill wouldn't make the optimum decision every time, as evidenced by their dealings with the Hammers. She could only try to do better the next time. She still thought the rest of her crew were idiots for putting her in charge. If they wanted to make the decisions, she would let them.

"I'm picking up communications between the advance

teams," Dorian announced as they entered a dock close to the arch-nest. They would have landed there when they were looking for the vault, but the schematics showed several choke points at which the Scourge could have set up defenses.

Desperation and the hope that their code broadcast would work had sent them back to the first dock. "The Hammers and Harvest are making good time. Facing a lot of Scourge on their way. We'll see how that goes."

"Someone's on our comm," she heard Blitz say over the sound of caster fire.

"That would be me," Chill announced, raising her eyebrows.

"Sorry," Dorian told her. "Might have accidentally connected to hear what they were talking about."

"That's not an accident," Kortez pointed out.

"Chill?" Blitz asked. "What the hell are you doing here?"

"Wondering why you thought it was a good idea to try to kill everyone on the station," Chill improvised. "That's on me, though. I forget that people do stupid things when they're not thinking."

"We thought about it a great deal," Blitz snapped. "We thought about how you were drawing mercs in to be cannon fodder for the Jindahin."

"There is no point in trying your mind games, mercenary." This one sounded like Hithaal, although it was difficult to tell over the noise in the background. "You betrayed those who put themselves on the line to fight through this station, and we're taking it back from you and your Jindahin supporters."

"Ah, yes. I should have known the Xo-Trang extremist

was the brains behind this." She would have to bring that up with the Over-Keeper. She'd really hoped he would do a better job of getting those assholes on their side. "So, your people sent you to try to take the station for yourselves."

"That's no different from you," Blitz stated.

Chill sighed as they headed back out. "If you had waited before heading out to get yourselves killed, you would have found out that the situation has changed. We found the treasure room and a way to inactivate the Scourge. After that happened, you would have received a lot more than whatever the Xo promised you."

"Don't try to bribe us," Hithaal snarled. "We had a tracker placed on your ship. We know where the vault is, and we sent a team to collect the treasure. In the meantime, we are attacking the arch-nest, and we will destroy the Scourge on this station once and for all."

She could have told him there was a genetic lock on the entrance that would stop any attempted incursion, but why offer intelligence to people who were intent on being their own worst enemies? They could deal with the Scourge bots and the plant infestation when they got there.

Chill still wanted to save their lives, but if the Harvest posed a threat to the entirety of the station, she would finish what she'd started when they arrived.

"Well, I'm sorry you feel that way." She drew her rifle from its holster as they went through the airlock into the station. "See you soon."

"What?"

"I'm sorry. I thought you had a tracker on our ship?" she asked sweetly. "Figure it out."

She killed the connection and set all their comms to a private channel.

"Sorry, boss," Dorian told her. "I should have caught onto them fucking us like that."

"Don't worry about it. We didn't think we would have to worry about a threat that wasn't the Scourge after the Sempers were put in their place. Nothing for it now but to learn from our mistakes and keep pressing forward."

Chill brought their group to a halt. "All right, we have to head back and help the Over-Keeper. Assuming the Xo get past the local wildlife, they could pose a problem for him, even with the pair of Janissaries at his side."

"They are here." Kuzratha's voice was garbled. It sounded like it was coming through interference, which explained why he hadn't alerted them about the developing situation. "They are trying to get through the door. I, my men, and the Treasure Keeper will have to make do. You need to go to the arch-nest to get the code in place. If they manage to take it down, there will be nothing to hold back the horde the Scourge is keeping at bay."

That was what the Treasure Keeper had assured them its purpose on the station was. Chill wanted to doubt the AI, but she had no choice now. They had to get to the arch-nest before the mercs, or they would have to find another central node. If the AI was telling them they had to succeed, or they would have a new enemy to face—one the Scourge was struggling to get past—she would listen.

As dangerous as the Scourge was, and as dangerous as the plants were supposed to be, the people they had thought were on their side had caused the most damage. She understood why the Hammers had gone over to the

Harvest, but she had hoped they would give her the benefit of the doubt.

If they wanted to resolve the matter peacefully, they had to get to the arch-nest before the Scourge or the plants killed everyone.

CHAPTER SIXTEEN

Chill didn't like the idea of leaving the Over-Keeper behind, although if the Xo made the mistake of killing him, they would be locked out of the vault. She wanted to know what Kuzratha would do. Either he would make a deal with the Xo, or he would die rather than give them what was his by birthright.

She couldn't imagine which one he would choose, although she thought she knew him better than most. His two Janissaries *might* be able to hold the incursion off, but she had to assume the worst.

"We've got movement ahead," Kortez announced, highlighting the point. They were in a labyrinth of hallways, which forced them to rely on Alex's directions and hope they wouldn't get lost. The AI was using the schematics they'd pilfered from the Jindahin, so they were likely to run into blockages in their way.

Ivan had enough explosives on him to clear anything from their path, and if that failed, the Janissaries were sporting rockets. If they ran into obstacles, they would deal with them.

"They're not attacking," Ivan pointed out. He kept his weapons trained ahead. "Doesn't look like they've noticed us."

She watched the five bots blocking their path—three of the rat bots and two of the felids. Scouts, but what were they looking for? They were deep in the territory taken over by the infestation, and with only five, they couldn't do much damage.

They were close enough for the Scourge creatures to pick up on them. They were already in visual range. Any other time, in any other place, the scouting team would have made a decision to back away or to attack, but neither happened. The patrol was moving right at them, but it wasn't clear if they saw the DEMC and the Janissaries as anything other than part of the station.

"The signal is working like gangbusters." Kortez was still pointing his rifle at the approaching bots. "You think it makes it so they just can't see us?"

"One way to find out." Chill stepped into the path of one of the felids. Its tail didn't glow, but it did notice her.

It stopped in its tracks, its photon receptors pointed at her and its mandibles making a series of clicks and chirps. It moved forward again and went around her, still chirping and clicking as the rest of the scouts moved down the hallway.

"I think it just told me off for getting in its way," Chill whispered, gazing after the bots. "The signal we're broadcasting is telling the Scourge we're friendlies. It might have been waiting for me to get out of the way, then it got annoyed when I stayed in place."

"Doesn't seem like an AI-run bot would get annoyed." It was the first time one of the Janissaries had spoken. "It was probably telling the nest running you to correct your coding."

"Plenty wrong with my coding." Chill smiled but kept her weapon on the bots until they were out of sight. Then she motioned for the team to keep moving. They were picking up more signals all around them, and as Chill adjusted her sensors, she identified the locations of the various patrols in the area. Not all of them, and some had weaker signals than the rest. She was tapped into the bots' communications to see where they were going. "Apparently, you need to have something wrong with you to be sent here."

"You think so?" Kortez asked.

She tilted her head and didn't fall over, though it took some fancy footwork. "Plenty of folks in the galaxy living normal lives. Accountants. Lawyers. Plumbers."

"Are those the three jobs that spring to mind when you think about having a normal life?"

"Sure. People go to work at the same time every day and go home to the same house, make the same meal—probably something healthy that's low in fat and high in fiber because they want to shit every day. Watch a retread vid and sleep in the same bed. That's the norm, or so I've heard. People who find themselves battling centuries-old bots and monsters created by biological weapons from the past in the far reaches of the galaxy have to have something wrong with them, right?"

Ivan chuckled. "Might be. Normal's overrated anyway. You think a normal person sees half the shit we have? Does half the shit we've done? Just because you're not cut out to have a boring fucking life doesn't mean something's wrong with you. You think building a station like this is normal? You think the people who did all this kept regular hours? There's a place for normal in the galaxy, but there's a place for the exceptional and the extraordinary, too."

It was a good point. Although the people who had run the early designs on the station probably *had* worked in offices and used supercomputers to calculate the variables.

She smiled. "Shoviil and the rest of the deckies trust us with their lives. They trust us enough to fight for us. Good to know we've earned it."

Shoviil appeared to think they were a better choice than the other mercs and was willing to risk his life on that theory. She would protect him and the those who followed him to the best of her ability.

"Nothing for it," Ivan agreed. "We have to head in there, defeat the monsters, and save the station. In short, be the big heroes we were always meant to be. You know, I think Albert Fonze should play me in the vid."

Chill tilted her head. "Fonze doesn't look anything like you."

"All the vid would do is have someone walking around in a stunt suit. All the closeups would be of him inside the helmet. Better to have people who look like him play the role, you know? Besides, they can do anything with makeup and implants these days, so they could make him look like me. What about the two of you? Do you want anyone famous to play you in the vids?"

"Fuck, no!" Chill cackled.

"You don't think there will be any vids?"

"Sure, there'll be vids, but I want to play myself. If anyone's going to be famous and make loads of creds for presenting a fictionalized version of my life, it's going to be me. Besides, they wouldn't need to get a stunt suit for it since I know how to run the suit."

Ivan coughed.

"Shut up," Chill growled. "I'm getting better, and by the time people cast for the vid, I'll be a wiz."

"I'll concede that."

CHAPTER SEVENTEEN

"What are we looking at?"

Chill had been afraid to ask the question since she thought she knew the answer. Their readings said it wasn't going to get any better. The Vert had been overrun by bots, which were poised to come at them from all sides. The whole chamber was the nest, so they would have to maneuver through it to find a node to work from.

"It's not the news any of us was hoping for," Kortez pointed out. "There are so many. I mean, we're broadcasting as friendlies, so they're not rushing in to kill us."

"Still don't think it's a good idea for us to wander in like we own the place," Ivan countered. "It worked on the small groups, but all it takes is for one smart bot to realize we're not bots, and the rest of them will be on us. You know all it takes is for one to get riled up to get the rest of them surging."

"Yes, we are aware of how networked intelligences work." Chill took a deep breath as she scanned the nest.

"We need to get to...I think this point. Lots of data streams crossing through there, so we can plug the fob in."

"There has to be another way in," the Janissary commander commented, pointing out a handful of spots on the schematics ahead of them. "If they pick up on us at those points, there will be no way to retreat. Too many points for them to hit us from on top, too. If we're discovered, this will not play out the way we need it to. Might be a roundabout path that leads us farther away from the central nodes, with fewer patrols for us to get caught up in. That reduces the chances of those patrols seeing through our clever disguise."

They needed to make a decision quickly. The longer they spent second-guessing themselves, the better chance the other merc assholes would have to assault the nest, and she knew it would not be a simple attack.

Not that they would listen if she warned them. Besides, one of the other crews might provide a distraction so her group could get out.

"There's a fucking army in there," Ivan whispered. He had finally gotten a decent look. "How the hell do they manage to power that many bots? They can't all have fusion reactors in them, can they?"

Chill shook her head. "You forget that the whole station draws power from the three massive fusion reactors outside. A lot of the power is going into the wormhole, but a tiny fraction will power billions of bots."

"Well, that's a nice thought," Kortez muttered. "We close to a decision?"

"We're going to take the roundabout way," Chill stated with a firm nod. "No point in braving the army of bots in there. We're going to play this slow and smart, and we'll have to hope our headstart on the Harvest and the Hammers is enough to get us where we need to go without much trouble."

Hoping hadn't worked out well for them so far, but she was going to keep doing it. She was an optimistic person.

"Let's get our asses moving." Chill started forward, and after a couple of heart-rending seconds, they fell into formation behind her. For a second, she'd feared facing the Scourge on her lonesome since her paranoia told her she wasn't the kind of person they would follow.

It did not take long for the first of their obstacles to get in the way.

"Big patrol," Chill whispered, raising an eyebrow. "I doubt we can just walk past them like the other ones."

Ivan shrugged. "What other option do we have? You want to turn around and find another way through? I mean, there's probably going to be something in our way no matter where we go."

He had a point. Chill did want to back off and find another way, but here they were. If they were going to piss off the Scourge, they should do that now so they could retreat to the ship and try again later.

However, if the Over-Keeper was to be believed, retreating wasn't an option.

"I might have something," Dorian announced. "I've been working on the code we got from the AI, and, well, I think I might have figured some of it out. Nothing groundbreaking, but if you aren't able to get around a group, I can try sending orders to move them into other areas. It won't work for larger groups, and it's more of a distraction. It might end up getting you killed, too."

"You might want to start believing in yourself, kid," Chill answered. "Show us what you've got. If there was ever a time to try something crazy and possibly stupid, it's now. Not ten minutes from now when we're surrounded by all the fucking bots on this fucking station."

That wasn't true. There were other nests on the station as large as the one they were in. However, from what the AI had told Kuzratha, losing one of the central nests would compromise the rest.

"All right," Dorian announced. "I sent the code, so it should be clear for you to move ahead."

A door opened next to the bots, and three of them turned to investigate. They didn't recognize the command and went on alert, looking for an intruder.

"I sense a weakness in this plan," Kortez commented. "If they're on high alert, won't they be *more* tuned on to intruders? You know, like us?"

"They're looking for intruders coming in by way of the door I opened," Dorian answered. "They're simple that way, but sure, there is still a risk. I assumed you were used to those by now."

"Big talk from the asshole who stayed on the ship." Ivan obviously had doubts, but he stepped forward, a knife in each hand instead of his rifles. The bots were still staring through the door like they were expecting someone to make an appearance. Dorian was right; they were simple, or at least single-minded.

They had to see the group stepping through their ranks, but the code kept the bots from redirecting their attention, which allowed the DEMC crew and their Janissary escorts to move through without being attacked.

Chill didn't give them cause to complain about her bad manners or whatever the felid had complained about.

Still, being among bots was never going to be a pleasant experience. Chill couldn't help but remember the times they had swarmed her, which made it difficult to think about anything but the positioning of the tails of the felids and those injectors the rat bots carried that would melt through her armor in seconds.

There weren't any of the larger bots, though. They might be too important to patrol the area, looking for organics to cull and purge from the station.

"You know, I've had nightmares like this," Ivan admitted, inching past the last of the patrols and slipping through the door before letting it close. "Waiting for the bots to attack and kill us all."

"Wouldn't the nightmare involve them, you know, actually killing you?" Kortez asked.

"Nah. I mean, yeah, they eventually get around to killing me, but that's where the nightmare ends, or right before. It's mostly being hunted by the fuckers. They know where I am, and they're just funneling me to where they will kill me."

Chill had those nightmares too, but she'd always managed to take control of them before they got too bad. She was good at creating and controlling her dreams.

Some people didn't have that ability, though, and Ivan was apparently one of them.

Chill motioned for them to keep moving.

"What, nothing to say about Ivan's dreams?" Kortez asked, falling into step with her.

"Nothing to say. We have this whole place hanging over us like a fucking sword waiting to fall. Sharing a station with horrifying killers is not funny."

Kortez shrugged. "*I* thought it was funny. Never had dreams like that myself."

"Fair enough." Chill smirked. "Then mocking Ivan is on you."

"No, it's not fun when it's just me."

"I can join in," Dorian chimed. "Don't have anything prepared, but let me think. Oh, right! I think Ivan might be a sex addict."

Chill would wait for him to get to the punchline before she told him it was a terrible joke.

"Because his biggest nightmare is being chaste."

She paused, then let out a cackle.

"I heard that." Dorian sounded smug.

"It was a terrible joke, but it did get a laugh out of me."

"That means it was a good joke."

"Nope, it just means I have low standards."

"We knew that about you, but...shit, hold on."

They didn't want to hear those words in the middle of the largest nest they had ever dealt with.

"What's going on?" Kortez asked as the group came to a halt. "Dorian, you'd better find the words to describe what's happening right fucking now."

"Nothing's coming for you, but the alert system in the station went up."

"Did we trigger something?" Kharkanaw asked, looking for what they might have tripped.

"No, nothing you guys did," Dorian answered. "Hold on, I'm checking. Oh, there we go. Looks like our merc friends just made first contact with the defenses. Not the whole group, just a dozen or so. Probably just their advance crew. Still, the whole nest just went on high alert."

"Nothing like knowing we have no time left," Chill muttered.

"There *is* good news. The fighting is drawing a lot of attention and most of the active bots, so the path toward the info node should clear out. As long as you don't, like, kick anything, you can keep moving. I'm opening the doors for you on the way."

Chill nodded and steeled her nerves. They had to go deeper into the nest and hope nothing crossed their path.

CHAPTER EIGHTEEN

"This is too easy," Ivan whispered, looking around. "It's too easy, right? When things go too smoothly, it means we're about to wander headfirst into a trap."

Chill was thinking the same thing. Saying it out loud felt like a jinx, but as long as she didn't say it, they should be fine.

The nest was larger than most buildings. It compared to the underground cities on Mugh-9, although it was eerily silent here, with only blinking lights telling them they were in an active nest.

They'd had to fight their way through a couple of patrols. Of the others, one had only realized the intruders were there when Chill accidentally shot one of them. The rest were more worried about the invaders on the other side of the nest complex.

"Too easy," Chill agreed. She looked around the chamber again. "Then again, we are working with the Scourge's core code. If there was an issue, we would be dealing with a much larger problem."

"What do you mean?" Ivan asked, narrowing his eyes. He was as cautious about their surroundings as Chill was, but he joined the conversation despite constantly scanning for patrols.

"It would mean we either have a rogue AI trying to take the station over despite its programming, or the Treasure Keeper severely underestimated how much its creation had changed and how fundamentally different it was from the source. Either way, it's the kind of problem we don't want to deal with. It's going to get all the anti-AI activists up in arms again.

"We haven't had a big AI controversy in the past few years, so they'll be aching to jump on this one. The Serpent will be quarantined, people will talk about how their parents or great-grandparents fought in one AI conflict or another, and they'll recommend that we bomb the station from orbit before it can cause any more trouble."

"You've spent a lot of time thinking about this," Kortez mused.

Chill shrugged, and her suit jumped at the gesture. "There isn't much for us to worry about. It's going to play out however it plays out. There's nothing we can do other than make sure that the fighting is all done on this end. If it's not, I say it's not our problem anymore."

"Way to toe the line between merc and hero there, boss." Kortez attempted to salute and accidentally punched himself in the head.

Chill grinned. "Hey, just because we're making the right decisions other people are too stupid to make doesn't mean *we* have to be stupid about it."

"How many people do you think we're going to have to

kill to save their lives?" Kortez countered. "I mean, we're walking into a fight with people too stupid to do what we're doing. Or too smart; I'm not sure which."

"Are you going to spend your time cracking wise, or are you going to do something?" Dorian asked over the comm. She wondered how he was keeping their communications from being intercepted by the bots. Even though it was a private channel, they would be aware of the signal going through the area. They would not be able to hear what was being discussed.

Maybe there was something to the code they were broadcasting that allowed him to mix it with the other signals going through the area. She would have hours of time to look through the code after the engagement. As old as it was, there was always more to learn, especially from some of the best and the brightest in the galaxy who had put their minds to making an AI that had done its job despite an infestation and fighting off pirates for decades.

It warranted further study.

"We're in the main nest, as I'm sure you're aware," Chill finally answered, glancing around. "We're looking for a node where there's a shit-ton of wiring to transmit commands all over the station. It's not like we got any instructions on how to use the code, so it probably we're just supposed to plug it in and...and..."

Her voice trailed off as she peeked over the edge of the walkway they were standing on. It was a few hundred meters above the bottom level, and looking down filled her with vertigo. It was made worse by the blinking, flickering lights that countered the darkness of the chamber.

That wasn't why she'd stopped talking, though. Chill

was looking for the source of another signal that was being sent under the transmissions from the bots. It was like a powerful OS was hibernating, and memories of the last time she'd seen something like it in a nest were coming up in her mind's eye.

"There," Chill whispered, highlighting the point the signal was originating from. There was nothing to indicate there was one of those big bots present, but there had been no sign of it the last time either...until there was.

Chill took a deep breath to keep her panic under control as she called up the readings from their location to make sure it wasn't an active ping. The Scourge wouldn't be able to mask that.

Like the last time, there was something curled against the pillars supporting the Vert, staying still and showing no sign of being a threat. Her mouth went dry when she saw the still form, and she clenched her fists as she backed away from the edge.

"That is bigger than the other one." Kortez had a talent for stating the obvious. "Three, maybe four times bigger. You think something that big can move?"

"It would be complicated," one of the Janissaries offered. "But possible. I read somewhere that they add grav generators to larger bots to make them less susceptible to failures in the grav systems."

"That's informative," Chill admitted. "But not relevant. I'm going to guess that those big fuckers operate as guardians for the nests in case anything gets through the outer defenses and they need to make a final push."

A last-ditch effort to defeat an attack. Chill didn't know if something that big could power up quickly enough to be useful in a situation like that, and she didn't want to find out.

"I have coordinates on a nearby point where we can connect the fob, and I can start uploading our AI's updates," Dorian announced, highlighting the point for them. "Seems like they're a few decades removed from their last core update. For some reason, that knocks all my electronics out until I update it manually, but something like this? Sure, it works perfectly."

It wasn't going to play out the way they wanted it to. Chill had come to terms with that. If Dorian was able to get the code in quickly, they wouldn't have to worry about what the Scourge was up to anymore. They would be able to focus on clearing the rest of the station. Then there would be a payday and their—in Chill's mind—inevitable confrontation with the Over-Keeper regarding the state of the station and what he had in mind for them for the future.

"We need to get this going," Chill muttered, approaching the point Dorian had highlighted. There were a variety of plugs for them to use, although she wouldn't just plug it into the first one. A couple were power nodes for the smaller bots—those too small to have their own reactors, like the rat bots. Information plugs were harder to find and usually in the center, where a variety of the bots could connect at the same time.

The clearest indicator was room around the plug to make space for the ports,

Chill slid the fob in and a green light glowed, telling her it was the right kind of point. She tapped the other points to see if there were any structural indicators so she didn't burn out the fob by plugging it into a power socket.

"All right, the code is uploading, and... Wow, that was fast."

Dorian shared what he was looking at to her screen so she could see what he was talking about. The core code was being rewritten, updated, and corrected in the spots where it had diverged from its core programming.

"What are we looking at?"

"Well, as you know, with fiber-optic cables, information is transmitted at the speed of light."

"I know that. I'm asking what kind of changes we're looking at since it's moving by too quickly to read."

"Oh, just...I don't know. You're better at this shit than I am, and this stuff is so old, I don't know what the hell the original code was meant to do."

" I can answer that," Kortez cut in as they moved down the walkway. They could hear the mercs and the deckies who'd sided with them fighting their way through the Scourge bots.

From the explosions and steady gunfire, Chill didn't think it was going well. Explosives were generally reserved for getting mercs out of trouble. She didn't know how the Hammers and the Harvest operated, but it was a general rule that most of the merc groups followed. Not for a moral reason. Explosives were expensive, so they were only used when hacking or shooting wouldn't be enough.

Though the fighting was intense, the bots were disengaging. They were pulling away from a group that was advancing through the chamber.

"I think it's working," Kortez growled. "Why are they still fighting?"

"If you think the mercs who thought they could charge in and take over the biggest nest in the area without recon have thought this whole situation through, you haven't been paying attention." The Janissary commander's disgust was clear.

"We need to go down there and let them know the situation is resolved," Chill announced. "The chances are slim to none that they'll listen to us, but we have to try to stop them from killing each other for no reason."

"I say let them die," another Janissary contributed. "They chose this path, and they knew what would happen if they antagonized the closest thing they have to allies on this hunk of metal. I say let them wake the big fucker up and get themselves killed. It'll teach them and the rest of the deckies a lesson about what happens if you split the group up. Kind of like the lesson you taught the Sempers, but more...permanent."

"The commander was the one who taught the Sempers a lesson," another chimed in.

She had gotten her wish; the Janissaries had joined their conversation and were communicating what they were feeling. She wasn't going to mention that in case they drew back again.

"We *are* going down there," Chill asserted. "If we can't convince them to call off their attack, we'll position ourselves to stop them from causing any damage to this Veil."

The Janissaries waited for their commander to concur, but she was going to leave with or without them. The

Over-Keeper had told her to keep everyone from destroying the Vert and the nest.

It would also be very bad if the Scourge didn't keep the other infestations down, now that they knew it was there to run interference for the people on the station.

If they had to fight the Harvest to prevent them from destroying their systems, she would. She'd keep the rest of the Harvest from joining their buddies on the station, too.

"Busy day," she muttered to herself as she connected her rope to a sturdy support that looked like it could take the weight of the suit.

CHAPTER NINETEEN

The code jumped from one bot to the other eerily fast. The bots had stopped attacking and were shuddering in place as the new code replaced the murderous sections.

Once that was finished, they went about their work like there wasn't a firefight happening around them.

It took the Hammers, the Harvest, and their decky friends a few ticks to realize something odd had happened. They were slow, but if Chill had been fighting for her life against a swarm of Scourge bots, it would have taken her a few beats to realize the situation had changed too.

They all looked around suspiciously, likely assuming it was a Scourge trick to get them to lower their defenses before the bots attacked again. They used the respite to check their weapons and armor and treat their wounded.

There were quite a few wounded since the fighting hadn't gone their way. Their aggressive attack, using the deckies and the Hammers as the head of the spear, followed by the Harvest crew, had gotten them deep into the nest…and isolated and in trouble.

It looked like half the deckies were dead or out of the fight. The Hammers had taken a couple of losses, as had the Harvest. Chill didn't know how many the latter had brought to the fight.

There were still enough of them to cause serious problems for Chill and her crew if they didn't believe her. They would not win if they charged into it headfirst. She marked the point where they could engage but keep the high ground. She wanted to believe all would be forgiven with the Scourge out of the action and nothing else threatening them. However, she would protect her crew in case that didn't happen.

It wasn't the best position, but Ivan was already lining his throws up. Kortez had identified a couple of shots as well. If this went sideways, they would need to take cover lest they were overwhelmed with fire from below. The Hammers only had casters for distance shooting, but the Xo's rifle slugs would penetrate their suits. The Janissaries might be able to withstand a couple of barrages, but then they would be out of it.

She had battle experience, but the Dahin Special Forces troops were professionals. Chill wouldn't tell them what to do unless they asked. The best way for the DEMC to make themselves useful was to draw the attention to themselves and let the Janissaries get into the kind of fighting they preferred.

Well, Chill didn't know if they preferred it, but they were very good at it. She wasn't sure if they laid everything out beforehand or if their training just kicked in when they were in the thick of it, but they smoothly set up their firing lines and created kill zones where they could inflict maximum damage without undue exposure.

She thought they would pull the same trick when DEMC was in the firing lines, so the three of them would learn from watching the Janissaries in action and find ways to exploit whatever weaknesses they had during after-action sessions—assuming they were still alive to hold them.

Chill left that to Alex. The AI would record and analyze the Janissaries' movements frame by frame to find a way to beat them.

That was tomorrow's battle.

Right now, Dorian and Alex were positioning the mechs on the upper walkways, sending ropes down for the DEMC trio. Some of the combatants were still wrecking bots, but the deckies had beaten a hasty retreat from the nest.

"The fight's over!" Chill announced. Her suit's speakers amplified her voice. "The Scourge has been reprogrammed to go after its original target, which doesn't include us. When it's done, we'll be able to shut it down and purge the real threat out of the station."

"You think we'd believe anything you have to say after what you tried to pull?" Blitz shouted, pointing his caster at her. "If what you're saying is true, the Jindahin will roll in and take over the station, leaving us with fucking nothing!"

Chill shook her head. "You don't have to believe me. All you have to do is fight for what you—"

Someone had taken a shot at her, and it had hit a lot harder than a caster round. One of the Xo rifles had hit her in the head, and she was lucky it hadn't taken it off. The armor was blaring alerts that told her that there was damage, although there was no breach. However, her ears were ringing, and she was nauseated.

The fight had started, but Chill took a second to recover before shooting back. It had been a cheap shot by the Xo. Smart, but cheap. Chill opened fire on full auto, anger bubbling up in her chest as she shot at those below.

Ivan's knives had dropped a pair of the deckies who were too slow to get under cover. With a smooth lob no one noticed, he sent a grenade into another position.

He was playing dirty too. Chill reached one of the ropes and shot downward to give her team time to get away since the Harvest was climbing up to the walkway they were perched on. The Janissaries had opened fire too. They knew that when their enemies reached the walkway, they were all going to die.

Twenty or so of the Harvest had survived the Scourge battle, and they sent their patsies in to take the damage for them while they rained rifle fire on the DEMC crew from afar.

The Hammers would jump into the thick of the fight at any moment, swinging their mauls and poleaxes. Those would damage whatever armor stepped into their way, although Chill was more than willing to pit herself against them.

She kept covering her team's retreat. "We need to change this up!" Kortez called after he hit the next walkway. "No point in running away from them. Eventually, we are going to run out of places to retreat."

"Not much we can do here," Chill commented as she tossed a grenade onto the walkway below to slow the advancing enemies. "This isn't our kind of fighting. We'll have to choose the points where we'll make our stands, then stick to cover and keep moving until the opportunity presents itself."

That would allow them to keep their options open. Any plan she could come up with would end up with them in a pitched battle with the Harvest.

Improvisation was key. She kept raining down shots down to keep the Xo from coming up. The Janissaries were also covering while Kortez and Ivan kept moving up. There were a couple of smaller exits they could use, but Chill didn't want to leave until it was absolutely necessary. The Jindahin wanted to keep the nest intact, which complicated matters.

If not for that, she would have headed back to the ship and ceded the position. They weren't in the martyr business. "Keep moving, keep shooting, and hope they fuck up."

Ivan nodded, tossed another of his knives, and caught the one he'd thrown before when it returned to him. "Sounds about right. Why do we always end up with a plan like that?"

"Because we keep rushing into fights we don't know if we can win for people who don't deserve our best efforts," Kortez pointed out. "I've been keeping track. Every crew we've worked with or for has tried to kill us at some point."

The math added up. Chill had blown a couple of those calls, but they had to keep their heads in this fight.

"We just need to keep fighting, stick together, and stay with the rest of our allies. We'll find a way out of this...*shit!*"

They'd been preoccupied with the Harvest making their

way up and hadn't seen the Hammers and their decky allies taking a roundabout path up. They were now on the same walkway as the DEMC.

"Commander, please keep up the suppressing fire on the Xo," Chill called over the comm. "We have a situation. Dorian, have the mechs fire down there too."

"You sure?" The kid had the sense to follow her orders while questioning them. "That'll leave you three fighting the Hammers and the deckies."

"We can hold our own."

Chill put more confidence into her voice than she felt. They *did* have enough firepower to pull it off, even with the numbers disadvantage. Still, it was three of them against two dozen at the very least. Heavy armor and coil-rifles would only get them so far.

"Ivan, use your knives and explosives in creative ways." Chill took a step forward and sent a salvo at the Hammers, who ducked behind pillars and returned fire.

"I know what to do," Ivan answered. "We'll have to draw them out of their cover, though. Get them to run at us."

"On it," Kortez growled. He drew Cortador and grinned as he slid the blade across his chest plate, creating a shower of sparks. "Come on, Chill. Let's show those Hammers the kind of mistake they made."

Chill couldn't help smiling. *This* was their kind of fighting.

"Come on!" she roared as she opened fire at the pillar two of the Hammers were using for cover. She and Kortez made their movements obvious. "Here's what you get for going against the Dead Evil Mercenaries, you fucking assholes!"

Kortez shouted something too, but she couldn't hear it. On the vids, hearing them yelling with Ivan on the backline would not indicate what they were trying to pull.

In their defense, Chill wasn't sure what they were trying to pull. She and Kortez had to draw attention to themselves as clear targets for their opponents.

Slugs pinged her armor. Chill kept firing even though each impact made her head ache. She obviously had a concussion, but there might be more damage. Her suit could stop bleeds and set broken bones, but it couldn't fix her throbbing head. She was going to kick the ass of the Xo who took that shot.

"Come out, come out, wherever you are!" she called sweetly as she fired two shots at the chest of a decky. She didn't know if they got through his armor, but the impact knocked him off the walkway.

That gave her and Kortez an opening to advance far enough that the Hammers would think they had overextended.

Out the Hammers came. Only three were left, and one was limping. Scorch—unless Chill missed her guess— had taken one of the rat bot's injectors to the leg. The acid had melted her armor and started on the flesh, although quick thinking had kept the injury from progressing too far. She could still fight, and she would probably keep the leg.

She wouldn't bet on surviving in a melee against those hammers, though. She really hoped Ivan did his thing soon.

Kortez did not share in her trepidation. He was spinning his blade in one hand and shooting with the other. He had taken the lead and charged Blitz and one of the others, knocking them back a step with his shoulder and slashing with Cortador.

Then the platform shuddered.

Ivan *did* have a plan. Blowing up the walkway with them on it counted as a plan, although she wished he had asked for her opinion. She wouldn't have been on board with it, but it did solve their problem of being in close combat with overwhelming numbers against them.

The walkway shuddered again as another explosive device went off, then the platform gave way, twisting and groaning under its own weight.

They all dropped together.

Maybe it had been a good idea. It was enough of a drop for their suits to prep for the fall and slow them down as they plummeted toward a lower platform. It was a lot sturdier than the walkways, supported as it was by dozens of pillars.

Still, it wasn't a pleasant experience. Chill hissed and groaned as her body was buffeted from side to side. She would have plenty of bruises and aches if she survived, but she supposed it was much better than how she would feel without the suit.

More importantly, it was much better than how the Hammers and the deckies felt when they hit the platform. A couple of deckies didn't make the platform and dropped to the bottom of the chamber. They screamed until they hit with loud wet thuds.

"That was your plan, huh?" Chill growled as she got up, then she sucked in a deep breath and tried not to let the nausea wracking her body make her puke. The Hammers had a hard tumble too, but Blitz had prepared them well.

All three had emergency thruster packs, and one had a grappler that slowed their fall enough to keep them alive and in the fight. Their comrades in arms fared much worse.

Blitz got his feet, flicked his hammer out, and activated it, then glared at Chill as she as took a step forward. She'd lost her rifle in the drop, and there wasn't enough time for her to draw her second one, so she raised her forearm. The heavy blow packed enough punch to force her to one knee, but she drew her knife and slashed at his hip to force him to take a step back so she could stand.

He closed quickly, moving faster than any other human she'd ever seen. That told her he was sporting combat implants. He leaped to her left, ducked her sweeping blade, and tried to grab the rifle on her back.

Chill was no slouch. She turned and knocked the weapon out of his hands before he could claim it. It was too large for him to carry comfortably, although he could fire at point-blank range.

"This is the future you see for the station?" Blitz snarled. He took a step back to catch his breath. He had been injured in the fall as well. "Destroying everyone who stands in your way?"

"I tried to stop you, but you took a cheap shot at me while I was trying to open a dialogue." Chill searched for her fallen rifles as she spoke. She could probably reach them, although she would take damage if he hit her with that hammer of his.

"The fight was over, but you kept fighting regardless. You're two down, and Scorch looks like she needs medical attention for her leg. Is that what you consider great leadership?"

"Am I supposed to look past what you were planning?"

"No!" She was tired of explaining herself. "You decided what was in the best interests of your team, but you should haven't let your feeling of betrayal and need for revenge guide you. They're looking to you for leadership."

He took a deep breath and glared at her, then lowered his hammer. "What would you have done in my place?"

"Honestly? The same thing. You have no reason to trust me, but I'm asking you to anyway. We stopped the Scourge from attacking, and we now know that there's a greater threat to this station. The Jindahin will need the help of the mercenaries and the deckies for decades or even centuries before they repopulate the station. Assuming the Xo will share the station after they take control of it."

"You want me to be a better leader than you are?"

Chill laughed. "That's not the highest of bars, but yes. For the good of your people, please stop this senseless fighting!"

She didn't know why she was trying so hard to make him see reason. Maybe it was because she felt responsible for bringing the Hammers to the Serpent, inspiring them to fight for their dreams, and then betraying them.

Maybe he understood why they'd done what they'd done, maybe he didn't. However, he had to know that if the fighting continued, they would lose more people even if they won.

"All right." Blitz powered his hammer down and hooked it to his belt. "You are right; we do not trust you. But this isn't our fight, and we didn't come all this way to hold grudges. There's not much money in that for the likes of us."

Chill nodded and took in a deep breath. The Janissaries were pushing the Harvest back, and the Xo were retreating to where the Hammers were standing.

"What the hell are you doing?" Hithaal snapped as he approached. "This isn't the time to exchange pleasantries. We have a fucking nest to destroy!"

"That's your business," Blitz answered, then motioned for the other Hammers to lower their weapons. "The Scourge threat is gone for the moment, and I won't commit any more of my people to your feud with the Jindahin. You do what—"

Chill saw it coming this time. The Xo had a penchant for shooting when their target was talking or negotiating. That tactic had earned them the unpleasant reputation they currently enjoyed.

As she rushed toward Blitz, three shots struck his chest. He stumbled back, and the rest of the Hammers were struck as well.

The Xo apparently didn't tolerate their "allies" deciding they didn't want to fight anymore. Chill dropped to her knees and used her suit's armor to stop more shots. It turned out shots to the back were less painful than shots to the head.

Blitz had fallen to his knees. She was too late. Three massive holes had been punched into his armor.

Blood ran from the holes as he sagged to the floor.

"Need...need to get clear," he whispered, gasping and coughing blood onto his helmet's visor. Chill guessed one or more of the rounds in his chest had clipped a lung, so he was drowning in his own blood.

"We'll get you out of here, Blitz. Don't you worry," she answered as she drew her sidearm and returned fire. The Janissaries were holding the rest of the Harvest off, but more rounds hit her shoulder and back.

"Not me," he whispered. "They have...rockets. If they couldn't get the countervirus into the Scourge system from here, they were going to blow the whole Vert. You need to get clear now!"

When Chill spun, she spotted three Xos setting up rocket launchers. There was nothing she could do. Ivan spotted them too and tossed a pair of grenades to try to stop them, but he was too late.

Smoke plumes left the tubes a few seconds before the grenades went off. The Xo with the rocket launchers were torn to pieces, but the rockets careened toward the pillars holding the ceiling up. She had a vivid recollection of the last time they'd blown a nest up, and the explosions were even more intense this time, taking massive chunks out of the pillars.

"Oh, you dumb motherfuckers," Chill whispered. She silently begged the pillars to hold, but they didn't. Their collapse was slow but inexorable, starting with a low cracking and creaking as the pillars sagged and crumbled. The platform shook as chunk after chunk hit it.

"The Scourge won't be a threat here anymore!" Hithaal declared, cackling like he'd just won a major victory. He probably didn't know that the damage he'd just caused would bring the whole Vert down.

Chill didn't have the time to explain it to him. She picked up the hammer Blitz had dropped. His body was limp, which told her he was either dead or close to it. The rest of the Hammers were in a similar state, leaving Kortez and Ivan with nothing to do but sprint toward more secure ground.

"You've killed us all, shithead!" Kortez roared at the Xo, who had realized that and was shouting orders to retreat at his men.

Not in time.

As usual, the grav was the first thing to go. Chill didn't feel her usual nausea, though. This time, all she could feel was the white-hot rage in her chest as her eyes locked on Hithaal. That asshole had just killed them.

She'd just told Blitz they weren't there to hold grudges, but maybe she could get one last thing right.

"Boss, your rifles!" Kortez shouted, holding them out to her. Chill was moving in the opposite direction.

The atmo was the next to go. There was a breach in the chamber, and the air was immediately vented to vacuum. The drag opened the holes wider, and the platform they were on started to shift.

"Disconnect!" Chill shouted. They needed to get away from the larger chunks. They didn't have much chance of surviving, but that was the rule when they were faced with explosive decompression.

Kortez and Ivan did as they were told. Everyone else who had survived jumped clear of the platform as well, aiming for the larger holes so they wouldn't bang around with the chunks being dragged out.

Chill had other plans. With Blitz's hammer in hand, she

watched as Hithaal followed his people and aimed his suit through a hole.

It seemed pointless since they were heading into the light of the system's three suns, but she felt like she owed Blitz revenge, and she would use his own weapon.

She rushed toward the Harvest leader, who suddenly realized he was being chased and tried to angle himself to get a shot off before she closed with him.

"Choke on this!" Chill screamed. The hammer powered up as she swung it with all the force she could deliver in mid-air.

It wasn't the kind of hit she had been looking for, but she got the effect she wanted. The generators in the hammer did their work, so the blow tore a chunk out of the man's armor, opening it to the vacuum he had created.

He screamed and tried to seal the hole as they were sucked through the bottom of the Serpent out into the pure silence and darkness of space.

There were worse ways to go. Worse places to go too. They had one hell of a view.

"Feel good about that, Captain?" Dorian asked over the comm.

"Got one last hit in," Chill whispered. Alarms blared in her suit, telling her it wouldn't be long before the pressure of the vacuum around her ripped it apart. "Get the ship out of here, kid. You and Ibu find yourselves cushy work in some area of the galaxy that's less horror-prone. Doesn't look like we're going to make it."

Kortez and Ivan were still alive if their suits were an indicator, but they were out in the vacuum too. Most of the Janissaries were heading toward the nebula. It looked big enough to swallow the whole galaxy, its tendrils reaching toward them like it was welcoming them.

" I guess I could do that," Dorian answered. "Or—hear me out—I could save your collective asses again."

A ping blinded and deafened Chill. Then she realized their ship was in space as well. It was too far away for her to see yet, but the signal was getting closer.

"Honestly, I have no idea how the three of you survived until I came along," Dorian muttered. "Anyway, get ready to be picked up. I expect hearty thank-yous when you see me."

CHAPTER TWENTY

"Looks like the station's holding up. That's a bonus."

Kortez found silver linings for every misfortune, and this was a substantial silver lining. There was evidence to suggest that if one Vert was damaged, the rest would collapse into the wormhole, but so far, the station had maintained its structural integrity.

There was no guarantee that it would continue to do so over the next few days, but if it failed, they would have enough warning to evacuate.

It wasn't the victory they had hoped for. The station was compromised, the nest was wrecked, and the Hammers were all dead. That had dawned on her when she reboarded the station. The whole grav situation was off, which she assumed was because a massive chunk of the station had been torn out.

Kortez was right. Not everything was bad. The Scourge had been reprogrammed, and her crew had made it out of the decompression alive. Chill hadn't thought they would, and it wouldn't have happened if Dorian hadn't been quick on the draw. He'd undocked their ship and picked them up before they were lost to the nebula. He'd managed to pick the Janissaries up too, as well as the empty mech suits.

Three of the Dahin Special Forces warriors hadn't survived. Their bodies had been collected from the vacuum, but one of them had sustained coilrifle injuries that had caused his suit to decompress, and the others had been struck by the flying debris as they exited the station, which had caused the same thing.

All that remained was for them to find out if the Over-Keeper had survived the attack on his vault. If so, they would get him and his two Janissaries clear so they could assess the damage and make hard decisions regarding the future of the station.

"Looks like they got into the chamber," Kortez pointed out. A couple of the Xo had been killed outside, and the plant infestation had started to reclaim the bodies.

The door was open, and an all-clear signal told them there were friendlies waiting in the chamber.

"Thank the heavens," Kuzratha murmured, shaking his head as he stepped out from behind a pillar. "Communications have been difficult, and I feared the worst."

"That would depend on your perspective," Chill answered as she looked around the room. The remainder of the Xos were scattered on the floor, and a few of them sported the bite marks Chill had seen when the commander had taken a Semper's head off.

The Janissaries had shed their mechs and the AI had controlled them, which had doubled their forces. The Janissaries had fought in their flight suits.

"Oh?" Kuzratha raised an eyebrow. He sounded concerned.

"The arch-nest was destroyed," Chill explained. The Treasure Keeper appeared next to the Over-Keeper. "And that Vert sustained heavy damage. The self-repair protocol might be able to work its magic on the sector, but it'll be a while before the area is habitable."

"The damage was far worse than you know." The AI's head hung low, and his tone was despondent.

"We lost the nest," Chill agreed. "But there are more of them out there, right? Plus, the code patch worked, so we don't have to worry about the Scourge anymore."

"True, but the destruction of one central node compromised all the others," the Treasure Keeper explained. "A great deal of data was lost, which is causing the rest of them to malfunction. They've shut their core systems down indefinitely."

"So, the Scourge on the rest of the station is defunct now?" Ivan asked, inspecting one of the bodies with bite marks.

"Yes and no." The AI seemed confused by the question. "The central nodes shut down automatically until they can be repaired, which won't be a possibility in the near future. The bots run on data loops that allow them to operate independently of the nests for short periods of time. It will take a while for those loops to deteriorate, but they too will shut down eventually. For the moment, they are focused on clearing the station of the mutant infestation, which should and already has put a dent into their advances across the station."

"How long until all the bots shut down?" Chill asked.

The Over-Keeper hadn't said much beyond his initial greeting, which worried her.

"It is difficult to say, considering how far along they have evolved past my initial development. A few weeks? Two months at the most. Then you will have to deal with the mutant threat on your own."

"Won't that be lovely?" She was still concussed, and although Zichix had treated her, a deeper scan and more tests awaited her when she got back to the ship. "Is there anything you can do to delay the situation? Keep the bots and the nests active until the mutants are cleared?"

" I will have to consider that possibility and get back to you. However, you will all have to come to terms with how the Serpent is changing. You will have to prepare yourselves for when the last of the nests go dark and the mutants learn that what has been holding them back is no longer there to stop them."

The AI didn't sound hopeful about finding a solution, which meant Chill probably couldn't either.

"Right," she muttered. "Well, we have to go back to Coil Cove and give the news to Shoviil and the crews. I doubt they'll take the news that the worst is yet to come very well."

The Over-Keeper nodded, patted Chill on the shoulder, and motioned for them to get on their way.

"Fucked this one up, didn't you?" Kuzratha began as they left the antechamber, locking it behind them so nobody could just wander in.

"I was unable to prevent others from fucking it up. That's different," Chill countered. "But yeah. We might ask why the Xo showed up to wreck the station, possessed of the firepower they needed to get the job done."

"I'll look into that." Kuzratha paused to eye the Dead Evil crew and his Janissaries. "There aren't many out there who could have done the job better than you did."

Chill nodded. She would make sure he paid them well, but there were still unanswered questions. She could guess, though. One theory was that the Xo had known about the dangers on the station and had come to stop those horrors from spreading to the rest of the galaxy, no matter whose hands it was in. Another was that they had been sent to recover Lugosh's weapons for the Harvest's purposes and failed miserably.

If that was true, more would come to finish the job.

Chill would consider what lay ahead for days if her crew let her. She was sure she could come up with a possibility that was worse than the current reality.

"You're doing it again," Ivan pointed out when they reached the ship.

"She's got the brooding look about her," Kortez agreed. "Shouldering the galaxy's problems and despairing that she can't solve them all."

"She's got half a mind to bitch-slap the pair of you," Chill countered with a grin. "Now, go help Ibu repair our suits. We're going to need all our assets sooner rather than later unless I miss my guess."

Kortez saluted. "Aye aye, Captain."

AUTHOR NOTES - MICHAEL ANDERLE

JULY 19, 2022

Thank you for reading this book and these author notes as well!

Dead Evil

So I had a reader mention that he felt it odd that I named this series "Dead Evil Mercenary Corps" and I'd like to set the record straight (or at least a little straighter) on my decision.

I have to admit part of it was just flat jealousy of some of the cool covers and series going around the time I named the series.

I can't even remember them, so I guess they weren't that amazing. Still, I felt this ragtag group of mercenaries and their attitude deserved a ******* name.

I knew our graphical artist, Jeff Brown, would create something incredible for the typography and wanted something just as bad*** for a name.

Oftentimes, I wonder if fans think that we consider long and hard what the name of everything is. I'm sure that I have done that within reason at times (The Kurtherian

Gambit, Oriceran, and others) come to mind. Still, this time it really had little to do with the big picture and more to do with *I just liked the name.*

I was running a little dry on ideas and started looking around. I looked toward Warhammer 40,000 (from Games Workshop®) for some inspiration at the time.

With the cool cities, whole worlds that were one big, massive set of skyscrapers, aliens out the wazoo, and armor that shrieked improbable if not downright impractical but cool as ****.

I wanted something like that too.

Once again, I completely admit that *jealousy played a part in this. I looked over the virtual fence at their cool **** and thought, 'why not me, too?'*

While we don't have the budget to do art in the style of Warhammer 40,000, I still admire everything they've done in that series.

I've never read a book, never played the game, pretty sure I've never played any of the video games. Still, I have been a fan of what it looks like and some of the visual concepts for a while.

I remember being in China a few years ago and seeing a Warhammer 40,000 diorama on display in a rather large bookstore. I was shocked as I didn't think some of our tabletop role-playing game systems would transfer over to China, and I found out just how wrong I was.

It helps that the main artist for these covers (Grimbro) is familiar with what I liked about the Warhammer 40,000 series and was able to give it a little panache in that arena. I hope you enjoy the artwork on the covers and the stories.

I look forward to talking to you in the next book!

Ad Aeternitatem,

Michael Anderle

P.S. Microsoft Dictation doesn't allow me to curse – it puts this shit "*******" in the paragraph.

MORE STORIES with Michael newsletter HERE: https://michael.beehiiv.com/

CONNECT WITH MICHAEL

Connect with Michael Anderle

Website: http://lmbpn.com

Email List: https://michael.beehiiv.com/

https://www.facebook.com/LMBPNPublishing

https://twitter.com/MichaelAnderle

https://www.instagram.com/lmbpn_publishing/

https://www.bookbub.com/authors/michael-anderle

Printed in Great Britain
by Amazon